OUR MANSION

ON ANGLIN' ROAD

a novel by Arthur Dale Likens

TATE PUBLISHING & *Enterprises*

Published by Tate Publishing & Enterprises, LLC
127 E. Trade Center Terrace | Mustang, Oklahoma 73064 USA
1.888.361.9473 | www.tatepublishing.com

Tate Publishing is committed to excellence in the publishing industry. The company reflects the philosophy established by the founders, based on Psalms 68:11,
"The Lord gave the word and great was the company of those who published it."

Book design copyright © 2007 by Tate Publishing, LLC. All rights reserved.
Cover & interior design by Lindsay B. Behrens

Published in the United States of America

ISBN: 978-1-60247-859-6
1. Young Adult Fiction   2. Christian   3. Family Values
07.09.28

Dedication

To my wonderful wife, Karen. Without your help and constant encouragement *Our Mansion on Anglin' Road* would not be a reality today. With all my love, I thank you.

To my beautiful daughter, Karina, and my handsome son, Dale. Thank you for your continuous support from the very beginning, many, many years ago.

To Patty Likens, my beautiful daughter-in-law and helpful editor. Thank you for all your expertise.

To Stefan and Griffin Koch, two of my six very special grandchildren! Thank you for listening to, commenting about, and assisting me each night we read *Our Mansion on Anglin' Road* together, before retiring to bed.

To Jake Likens, another very special grandchild! Thank you for being the very first to read *Our Mansion on Anglin' Road* in its final version and lifting my spirits with your gracious comments.

To all my friends and family who have kept the fires burning with your everlasting encouragement throughout the years.

To Mom, Dad, and all my brothers and sisters.

To Bill Nelson and Johnny Sanchez, my dearest friends and neighbors from Anglin' Road.

To my brother Gene. This is your Story!

Arthur Dale Likens

Acknowledgement

A special thanks to Tate Publishing & Enterprises, LLC. Without you, *Our Mansion on Anglin' Road* would still be only a dream.

Thank you, Allison Johnson, Lindsay B. Behrens, and all who contributed to the publishing of this book. Your patience and sincere dedication will always be treasured.

Thank you, Richard Tate, for your kind words and belief in *Our Mansion on Anglin' Road*.

Thank you, Dale and Patty Likens, for your desire and ability to pursue my long-held dreams when I was unable to carry on.

Table of Contents

Foreword 11

Preface 13

1 | A New Family 15

2 | "It's God's Will!" 21

3 | Anglin' Road 27

4 | The House On Anglin' Road 29

5 | Henry's Frightening Ghost Story 37

6 | The Singing School Bus 43

7 | "You're Too Small to be in School!" 51

8 | Herb Fights Back 57

9 | "A Woman's Been Murdered in Our Woods!" 63

10 | Betty Jane 73

11 | The Best Farm Around 79

12 | Teddy—A Gift From God 89

13 | The Bear That Stalked Anglin' Road 97

14 | The Strange Intruder 103

15 | The Stranger 109

16 | Dad's Pride 115

17 | Uncle Clyde Nearly Drowns 123

18 | Christmas Preparations 131

19 | Reindeer on the Roof 143
20 | Christmas Day. 151
21 | Glen's Illness. 161
22 | 'Pillow Talk' 171
23 | Medicine From Uncle Slim 175
24 | Showers of Blessings. 179
25 | A Terrible Thing Happens to Betty Jane 183
26 | "It's Larry Vincent From 'Pillow Talk!'". 193
27 | Dad's Slipped Disc 203
28 | "Good ol' Aunt Rose!" 213
29 | Pastor Wiggins 221
30 | The Musical. 229

Foreword

Welcome to *Our Mansion on Anglin' Road,* a heartwarming and poignant story of a large blended family living in Ohio. Prepare to be captivated by the characters and stirred by their determination. From the magic of a lucky stone to an unshakable faith in the goodness and providence of God, their triumphs and defeats will refresh your spirit. This is an enjoyable book, a journey into the lives of a family whose values and morals are as American as apple pie. Arthur Dale Likens is the talented artist who paints the picture of a family striving to live every day with a God-consciousness that makes the difference for each of them as individuals.

Mary Perdue
First Lady of Georgia

Preface

I was born in Sharon, Pennsylvania, just before America entered WWII. I remember, vaguely, the food rations, the blackouts, and my Uncle Ray being sent to Pearl Harbor. But most of my early memories center around a small, Ohio town named Hartford. It was there that my mother and new stepfather decided to settle and rear their family of eight children. There, on a lonely, dusty road, far from civilization, my wonderful journey through childhood began and ended.

In Our Mansion On Anglin' Road, I prove that children will always endeavor to choose good over evil when led by loving parents. Hard times build character, endurance, and strength. Being poor is only in your mind. And true love and joy in life are not just physical, but dwell in the hearts of all who truly care for others.

Arthur Dale Likens

1 | A New Family

"Good Lord above!" Uncle Clyde shouted as he ran toward my new stepbrother, Henry, who was dangling at the end of a long rope he had attached to the barn's hayloft above. "I don't think that boy has the brains he was born with!"

He ran past Mom and my brothers and sisters and me as we looked on in complete surprise. Quickly, Uncle Clyde climbed the steps leading to the barn's hayloft.

Looking down at Henry, he placed his hands on his hips and shouted angrily, "What in the world are you trying to do?"

"I was tryin' t'get t' the groun' by tyin' the rope 'round my waist!" He gasped as the rope squeezed tighter.

"For Pete's sake!" Uncle Clyde hollered down. "You have to make sure the rope is long enough to reach the ground! Any idiot could figure that out!" He shook his head in disgust. "If it wasn't for your mother's sanity, I'd let you dangle there until the cows come home!" But he did pull Henry to his safety.

Henry quickly pulled his shirt over his head, rubbed the burning rope marks vigorously with it, and smiled down to us as though he were some kind of hero. That's when Aunt Rose grabbed him by his ear and twisted it until it nearly bled. "You do that again and I'll paddle you until Lake Erie dries up!" she bellowed.

Not long before Henry nearly hanged himself, Mom, Glen, Esther, Roberta, Robert, and I were living with Grandma and Uncle

Slim in Sharon, Pennsylvania. Mom called us all into Grandma's parlor.

"Gather around me, children," she said. "I've got something important to tell you all." Before we could even imagine what it might be she smiled and said, "I'm getting married again."

"Married!" My older brother, Glen, shouted. "You're getting married again?"

"Yes, I'm getting married again."

"I didn't know you were serious about anyone, Mom!" Esther said.

"Well, I am. And we've been planning this for a few weeks now. Your new stepdad's name is Randall Stevenson. You will always call him Dad from now on," she said. "And he's bringing his three sons into our new family. Eddie is just a few months older than you, Carl," she said as she looked straight at me.

"Three more brothers?" Roberta interrupted.

"Yes, Roberta. Three more brothers."

"Three more brothers," Roberta repeated sadly.

"And Wesley is two years younger than you, Carl," Mom continued. Then, I think she tried to warn us about Henry, but she didn't quite have the words. She just said, "Henry, well, Henry…" Then she paused and looked to Grandma and Uncle Slim who were standing by the door. "Well, Henry's a little mischievous!"

Glen squirmed in his wheelchair. "Oh, great! Just what we need in our family, a trouble maker!"

"Now I didn't say he was a trouble maker!" Mom was quick to respond. "I only said he was mischievous."

"Well, anyhow, do you mean we'll have to change our last name now?" he asked. "Now that you're getting married again."

Mom smiled and said, "No, Glen, you'll always keep your last name."

"At least that's some relief," Glen said. "I like our last name, *Lovegood*."

I looked back at Grandma. She took a small handkerchief from her apron pocket and dabbed her eyes softly.

Soon after that, we kissed Grandma and Uncle Slim goodbye. Grandma cried and dabbed her eyes with that same tiny handkerchief. Then, with our new dad and new brothers, Henry, Eddie, and Wesley, we moved to that tiny house in Brookfield, Ohio.

Uncle George was Mom's younger brother. He wasn't happy about Mom getting married again. I heard him laugh in a sarcastic way and say, "If that marriage lasts one year I'll shave my head and go bald the rest of my life!" I didn't like what he said, but I laughed at Uncle George being bald the rest of his life.

Shortly after Henry nearly hanged himself, Dad came into the house and simply said, "Pack your bags, everybody. We're movin' to a large, old farmhouse in Hartford, Ohio."

"We jist got here!" Henry belted out. "Why in the world are we movin' so soon?"

Dad just looked at Henry, as though he was going to say something nasty, then he smiled and said, "'Cause I'm afraid you'll *really* hang yourself if we stay here any longer."

"Hey! That's great! We're gonna move again!" Robert said.

"What's so great about that?" Roberta answered.

"Yeah! What's so gate 'bout that?" Wesley agreed.

"Never mind," Mom said. "Your dad has a good reason and that's all there is to it." She moved to Glen and leaned against his wheelchair. "I sure will miss Rose and Clyde," she said. Then she lifted her apron to her eyes and quietly left for the kitchen.

Aunt Rose and Uncle Clyde weren't really our aunt and uncle. They just lived across the road and claimed to be our long lost aunt and uncle. For some strange reason, each of them loved us as though we were their own children. Mom said it could have been because they couldn't have children of their own. Then she grinned and said, "Then again, maybe they're just crazy."

Aunt Rose was the meanest, toughest, and bossiest person I have ever known. She was so mean she could scare a coon out of a tree at night, Dad once told us. Dad also said that if a fight ever broke out he wanted Aunt Rose on his side. She had the strongest grip, the fastest legs, and the loudest yell of any woman west of the Allegheny River. When she put her two little fingers into her mouth to whistle for our attention, every dog for miles around began wailing in complaint. With her bleached blonde hair, her broad shoulders, and a cigarette dangling from her bright, red lips, Aunt Rose demanded attention from my seven brothers and sisters and me and by golly, she got it.

But Mom said Aunt Rose was also the most loving and kindest person she had ever known. When the chips were down, as Mom used to say, it was Aunt Rose who was always there. Mom said she would miss Aunt Rose more than anyone else when we moved to Hartford.

I remember Aunt Rose's first words to Mom when she took one look at the eight of us children. "Good God above, Lydia, I'll help you raise that brood of heathens if it's the last thing I do in this world!" From that moment on, Aunt Rose began twisting our ears, pulling our hair, and shouting out orders.

The very day we were moving to Hartford, Aunt Rose stood beside our Willys, parked in the driveway. "I'll be there as soon as you get settled in, Lydia," she promised Mom as the January snows began to fall harder and harder. "By golly, I'll straighten those brats out or my name's not Rose Toby!" Then she reached through the back window and twisted Henry's ear.

"You behave yourself, young man, or I'll tan your bottom until you see stars when I visit you in Hartford! Do you understand me?" Then she twisted Henry's ear harder.

"Yes, Aunt Rose!" Henry bellowed.

"And that goes for the rest of you heathens, too!" She sneered at each of us crammed on top of one another in the back seat of the Willys.

"Yes, Aunt Rose!" we answered quickly.

Uncle Clyde stood beside Aunt Rose and broke into laughter that shook his entire body. He reached down to his pants and pulled them up with his wrists. As Dad drove the Willys out the long driveway, I looked back and saw Aunt Rose wiping her eyes with the sleeve of her winter coat. Uncle Clyde stood beside her waving goodbye.

2 | "It's God's Will!"

Glen sat between Dad and Mom in the front seat of the old Willys. Mom spread a blanket across his lap and tucked it firmly around his weakened body.

"It's God's will!" Esther beamed behind her pretty smile. The Willys bounced and swayed through the brisk, January breeze while large, fluffy snowflakes zipped toward the windshield and then suddenly darted away. "That's why we're moving," she continued, though few of us barely acknowledged that she had even spoken. Our eyes and minds were glued to the enchanting, strange scenery slipping quietly by the windows of the Willys. "Someday, we'll know the reason why."

I stared out the window of the Willys, across the snow-covered ground. Although I said nothing, Esther's words raced through my mind over and over again: "Someday we'll know the reason why." At times I had wondered why we were moving. I remembered Mom, on occasions, saying we didn't have much money. Maybe our new home wouldn't cost so much. And I also remembered Dad saying he needed to get out in the 'sticks' where he could be free like he was on the farm he knew as a kid; where he could farm and trap and hunt and fish. I glanced at Mom and I could tell by the look on her face that she was proud of Esther's comforting words. It was just like Esther to console the rest of us at a time like this.

That's when Henry busted in. "How come you know so much 'bout God?" he snapped bitterly.

"Because I talk to Him! That's why!" Esther quipped in retaliation.

"And I suppose He talks t' you, too!"

"Of course He does. He'd talk to you, too, if you'd just open your ears!"

"Oh, sure! I suppose He'd say, 'Good mornin', Henry! How are you t' day?' 'Oh, I'm jist fine, Sir! An' how are you?'" Henry mocked in a raspy voice.

"Well, He just might if you'd give Him a try, smarty pants! Besides, that's sacrilegious to make fun of God!"

"All right! That's enough now!" Mom shouted and snapped her head around to face the two.

"Well, he is sacrilegious! He ought to be ashamed of himself!" Esther fumed.

"Well, you act as though nobody wants t' move. I'm not afraid t' move. I'm gonna like livin' out in the woods with no runnin' water or electricity. Just because you're a sissy and can't take it..." Henry stopped suddenly this time because Mom whirled around quickly and glared angrily at Henry and Esther.

It was true that some of us had not wanted to move. Wesley hid in the hayloft that very morning and said he was part of the ol' homestead and would surely die if he had to move from it. Roberta cried the night before and said she didn't want to move. But everyone knew Roberta just wanted to be different from Robert. Since they were born twins, Mom said they were born to disagree. Once, Roberta argued that she was born first, "Because all good things come first!" But Robert simply responded with, "I shoved you out first so you could go and prepare the world for me!"

But just the other night, I thought Glen was going to burst like a bubble when Mom told of the famous musicals held every other year in that small town of Hartford. "Word is, they only accept the best performers in the area. And they haven't heard the best till they've heard you and the girls," Mom boasted to Glen.

From that moment on Glen's eyes lit up like all the stars in the sky. "You can do anything in this world, if you want to," he told me. "And what I want most right now is to sing in that musical!"

When Glen told me that I went right outside that night and found the prettiest lucky stone I could find. Grasping it tightly in my fist, I held it up to the millions of twinkling stars above my head and wished upon those stars like I never wished before. I said:

"Star light, Star bright
First star I see tonight
I wish I may, I wish I might
Have the wish I wish tonight!

"And my wish is that Glen will someday sing in that wonderful musical. Please, dear God!"

Then I took that lucky stone and rammed it deep into my pocket so I would never lose it. And I promised right there and then that I would never let that lucky stone go until Glen's dream came true. No, sir! I would keep that stone forever, if I had to, because recently Mom had said that Glen's health was slipping day by day. If he ever got too sick or too weak he would never be able to sing in that musical.

Now, as I sat in that old Willys with my seven brothers and sisters and Mom and Dad crowded in around me, all I could think about was Glen. "You're just like Glen in so many ways," Mom told me one day.

And she knew that's just what I wanted to hear, too. I wanted to sing like Glen. I wanted to draw like Glen. I even wanted to look like Glen. But I didn't. Glen had dark brown hair that laid flat across his head. My hair was light brown and curly, like Robert's.

Glen's ears were small and looked like they were pinned to the sides of his head, but mine stuck out at the top. His eyes were tiny slits across his forehead while my eyes were round as saucers, like Esther's.

One day, when Glen was real sick, Mom told me all about muscular dystrophy. "He's already lived longer than most people with muscular dystrophy," she explained. "Every day means so much to him. One day is like a year to him." And that's why I knew it was so important for Glen to stay healthy; so he could sing in that musical.

Suddenly, Dad brought the Willys to an instant halt and we all flew forward. "Look t' the left, everybody!" he commanded.

"O-o-o-h!" Wesley whispered and gasped for air.

"Aren't they beautiful?!" Roberta exclaimed.

"They sure are!" Glen agreed.

There, in a small grove, nestled in the thicket of a few long-needled pine trees, stood six of the most beautiful deer our eyes had ever beheld. Beneath the lofty branches, heavy laden with fresh snow, a silver tunnel wound through the thick trees. From within the tunnel two fawns flounced forward on spindle-legs and pranced awkwardly toward the others. Not caring that an innocent move might alert their common predator, they were free to roam among the hemlock spruce and toss their gangly bodies in friendly play. Nearby, the older deer watched with quick eyes and pointed ears.

"They're probably searchin' for food," Dad said. "It's very hard for deer t' find any food in the woods in this kind of weather."

Suddenly, one buck, who must have been the leader, jerked his head at the purr of the Willy's engine, and after a moment of suspended action, quickly bolted toward the north woods. Immediately, as though it had been rehearsed time and time again, the remaining deer responded to his signal and swiftly sprinted behind their leader. What a resplendent sight it was to see their tiny, white tails bob and bounce through the woods, leaping over scratchy blackberry bushes, and kicking their heels high behind them as they seemed to glide to safety in the dense woods that lay ahead!

"They're so beautiful! So beautiful!" Esther whispered. "I don't think I'll ever see anything that beautiful again!"

"Well, they're gone now," Dad said as he pulled the long gear stick into first gear and once again proceeded down the road. "But I'll bet you're wrong, Esther. I'd be willing t' bet we'll see plenty more deer before the year is over." Dad smiled now and settled back into his seat. And though the Willys continued to swerve and sway past the ruts and through the deep snow, as though Dad's full attention was on the road ahead, it was quite obvious to me that the sight of the deer had aroused his memories. His glassy eyes and faraway look told me that Dad was thinking, once again, of his early childhood days back in the Boys' Home in northwestern Pennsylvania. So many times I had seen that same distant look on Dad's face. How often he had told us of the times he and the other boys of the Home had watched the deer come to the babbling creek behind the Home to lap the cool, refreshing water. How still they sat, barely breathing, careful not to make a sound or a move for the deer might quickly slip away!

The Home had meant so much to Dad. It was there he, and the other boys, freely roamed the woods and learned to trap, hunt, and fish. It was there, he had learned the very rudiments of life. He had learned to build things, repair things, and even make things that had never been made before. It was there, too, that Dad had been instilled with a love for the land around him. He had learned to farm the land, cradle it, and respect it, for it had become his life. It was no secret to us children then, that part of the reason for the sudden plans to move to Hartford was Dad's deep longing to return to the land, to plant his roots so deep they could never be pulled out.

Mom, on the other hand, had been born and reared among the crowded buildings and back alleys of a small metropolis. Little did she know of the wide, vast country that surrounded that city, for hers was a life of noisy neighbors, streetlights, and factory whistles. Until she had married Dad and moved to Brookfield she had not known the sweet fragrance of honeysuckle on a cool spring morning or the mournful sound of a turtledove calling across the meadow to its mate. But Mom knew what it was to work. As a young girl of ten she found herself cleaning houses for neighbors for a meager dollar a week. And that dollar was quickly given to her mother to help support her younger brothers and sisters because a thing called the Great Depression had spread like wildfire across the country causing many fathers to lose their jobs.

But that was all in the past. And though these were difficult times, too, Mom and Dad had often told us children that great lives are often molded in difficult times. "Only the Good Lord could foresee what good could come from the life that now lay ahead," they had said convincingly.

3 | Anglin' Road

Surprisingly, everything became unusually quiet in the car. For the moment, Henry and Esther were content to enjoy the strange, new scenery slipping by our windows. On each side of us a wall of snow-covered trees towered high above while the Willys chugged slower and slower down a narrow path Dad said was Anglin' Road.

"It looks more like a cow path to me," Roberta whispered sarcastically under the purr of the car's engine.

The blustery winds whipped the snows harder and as they zipped past the windshield of the Willys, a peculiar secrecy about this road captured my thoughts. I felt as though we were trapped in a time machine stepping back into time; a time even before Mom's and Dad's. Then the fighting started all over again.

"Wow! I'll be a monkey's uncle!" Henry shouted. "There's the wooden bridge you said was by our house, Dad!"

"Holy cow! You're right, Henry! Finally, you and I agree on something," Esther quipped. "Not that that's a wooden bridge up ahead, but *that you're a monkey's uncle.*"

Once the laughter had ceased and Esther had brushed the proud tears from her eyes, Roberta joined in. "That sure was a good one, Esther!"

"Not bad for a baboon!" Henry said in retaliation.

"That's enough of this name calling!" Mom interrupted. "Both of you, now!"

"Well, a baboon's homelier than a monkey's uncle anyhow," Henry said faintly.

"Sounds like you're admitting that you *are* a monkey's uncle to me!" Esther squeezed in once more with upturned nose.

"I said that's enough!" Mom called again.

"Baboon's still homelier than a monkey's uncle," Henry whispered under the purr of the car's engine.

"Tis not!"

"Tis too!"

"Tis not!"

"Tis!"

"Tisn't!"

"For cryin' out loud!" Robert interjected angrily. "I don't see where either one would win a beauty contest!"

"Makes no difference what you think anyhow," Henry complained to Robert. "You're just a monkey's brother anyhow!"

"*That proves it now! That proves it now!*" Esther squealed with delight. "*If Robert's a monkey's brother, just what does that make you since he's your brother?*"

All around the laughter grew louder now. Perhaps Henry could have kept the argument going even longer had he said what I was afraid he would say. But even Henry knew better than to say Robert wasn't really his brother, that he was only a stepbrother. That's when Dad stopped the Willys smack in the middle of the road and turned to face us all. "If I hear another word from anybody in this car I'll tan every last one of you! Do you understand?"

I didn't understand why I would be tanned for what Henry and Esther were saying, still I chorused in with all the others and said, "Yes, Dad."

After a few moments, Dad finally slipped the gear stick into first gear and slowly the Willys chugged across the old wooden bridge. "That's Yankee Creek," Dad said in a much softer voice as we passed over the frozen creek below. "And right here is our new home." Quickly, he turned the Willys to the right and up a small hill.

4 | The House On Anglin' Road

Against the pale, gray sky, resting on a small hill, sat an old, grayer house, torn through the ages, weather-beaten and feeble. It was the largest and most run-down house I had ever seen. From the high windows, loose shutters hung feebly, banging with the slashing winds. Here and there detached boards sprang from the aged house. High above, clinging hopelessly from the overlapping eaves, a rusted rain gutter swayed with the brisk winds and prepared for its eventual fall to the earth below.

"It looks like it's been deserted for years," Eddie said as we all stared mysteriously at the worn-out building that now loomed in front of us.

"What does 'serted mean?" Five-year-old Wesley asked wearily.

"It means there are prob'ly ghosts in the house," Henry replied softly and chattered his teeth as though he himself were terrified at the ghastly thought.

"I don' like it here!" Wesley said frightfully, slipping into Roberta's strong hold.

"It doesn't mean there are ghosts in there and you know it!" Esther quickly replied. "It means *nobody* lives there and that includes ghosts!"

"It looks like a mansion t' me," I said.

"A mansion?" Henry laughed and turned to look at me. "Do ya have any idea what a mansion looks like? If that's a mansion, I'll eat my socks." Then Glen, Esther, Roberta and Robert all began to laugh.

"That ain't no dumb mansion for sure!" Robert snickered.

Mom studied the house now with searching eyes. Gently, she doubled the quilted blanket across Glen's legs and tucked it firmly under as though she must begin immediately the difficult task of sheltering his weak body from this old, broken-down house.

"I know it's pretty obvious," Dad said as he leaned across Glen to get a better look at the old house, "but nobody has lived in this house for a number of years." Then there was dead silence throughout the car while each of us studied the house intently. "I know you can't understand it by lookin' at that run-down house in front of you," Dad spoke again, "but I believe that house is gonna be a blessin' t' all of us. Clyde an' I looked it over a few weeks ago. There's coal in the cellar, an' there's some old, but solid oak furniture in the house."

"And God bless Rose and Clyde," Mom interrupted. "They brought some bedding out a few days ago and cleaned and set the house in some kind of order."

Then, scanning the vast domain that lay outside our car, Dad said, "An' best of all, there are seventy-five acres of land here! Do you know what we can do with seventy-five acres of land!? Why, we can have the best farm around! An' the best part is, it's only gonna cost us twenty-five dollars' rent a month!"

I couldn't explain it then, but the excitement I heard in Dad's voice sent chills down my spine. The moment I stepped out of the Willys and into the snow, goose bumps as big as my knuckles pricked my skin all over my body. At first, I stared at that old worn-out house, then my eyes seemed glued to the magnificent barn out back. When I turned and faced the old pump beside the barn, I thought its handle was waving hello to me. Finally, I spotted the tiny building Mom had told us was our outhouse and my heart began to beat faster and faster.

The bitter, January winds whistled through some dead apple trees near the driveway, while large snowflakes fell softly upon my face. Across the driveway and behind the house, the door of the tiny outhouse banged back and forth. I saw a seat with two holes. Snow covered the entire floor and swirled in small eddies. A rusty, barbwire fence lay broken and coiled at the first rotted post behind the outhouse. A smaller pump stood near the backside of the worn-out house; its handle jutted out of a large snowdrift like a frozen, outstretched arm. Like the larger pump, near the barn, its handle reached out, as though to shake my hand, welcoming me home.

Strange-looking farm tools filled an open shed on the opposite side of the driveway. Small black birds darted in and out of the large open doors of the barn loft. I ran to Anglin' Road and looked back to where we just came from. Not a house could be seen. Quickly, I turned and looked the other way. Not a house could be seen as far as I could see. Not a soul lived anywhere near us. We were all alone.

"Carl! Come on now!" Mom called through the bitter winds. "I don't want you getting an earache in that cold air. And Henry, you and Robert untie Glen's wheelchair from the back of the car."

So, one-by-one, we smaller children and Mom followed Dad as he carried Glen up the steps of the decrepit side porch while Henry and Robert followed behind with Glen's wheelchair.

Mom reached the door of the side porch, twisted the handle and gave a nudge with her hip. The door gave a loud screech, opened part way and then stopped. With a quick thrust of her shoulder the door flew open with a loud burst and banged against the inside wall of the kitchen. Momentarily, she stood at the threshold adjusting her eyes to a sudden burst of sunlight that lighted the entire kitchen. Then, remembering that Glen was still in the cold air, she quickly moved inside to allow Dad and Glen to enter.

While Dad set Glen carefully into his wheelchair Mom searched the vast room in which we now stood. It was an unusually large room with an old, oaken table sitting precisely in the middle of the room. Against the east wall was an aged wood stove.

Mom took a coiled metal handle and pried a small, iron plate from the stove. "You just burn wood or coal under these plates and set your pans of food over the holes," Mom said. "The fire will heat the food in the pans above. How well I remember my grandmother cooking on a stove just like this."

There was a wooden sink with a small pump that led directly to a cistern just outside the north window. Dad grabbed the short handle and pumped it up and down. Ice-cold water flowed from the mouth of the pump. "I guess Clyde primed it when he an' Rose were cleanin' house. Lord only knows how many years it's been since it last saw water."

Adjacent to the kitchen, a large pantry revealed hundreds of empty, quart jars neatly arranged on dusty shelves. From inside the pantry a door led to the cellar. As Dad opened the door, grand-daddy long-legged spiders swung back and forth on sticky cob-webs. "I'll go down an' stoke the furnace, Lydia. You go ahead an' look the house over with the kids."

Together, we followed Mom through each of the large, empty rooms as she pushed Glen ahead. The hard wood floors cried loudly with each thump of our heavy boots while the thin walls echoed our every word. Mom studied each room carefully. Then, returning to the room beside the kitchen she said, "I guess this will be your Dad's and my bedroom. The room next to it is much larger. It will be our living room."

"What about Glen, Mom? Where will he sleep?" Esther asked.

Mom looked to Glen and then from the corner of her eye she caught Wesley playing in the fireplace. "Wesley, for Pete's sake, get your hands out of that fireplace! You'll have soot all over you." Wesley wiped his hands on his coat and moved back from the fireplace. Mom's eyes were now focused on the sooty walls of her bedroom. "Well, I guess he'll be sleeping in the only room left downstairs. Lord knows it's far too cold upstairs." She looked now to Glen and pulled the blanket over his shoulders. "Besides, it will be next to impossible to carry you up and down those stairs twice a day, so you'll sleep in the room behind the living room."

Fancy wallpaper from another period of time adorned each of the rooms. Dusty cobwebs Aunt Rose and Uncle Clyde must have missed hid at the ceilings where the walls met. There were no light switches because there was no electricity in the house. In each of the rooms fancy, wrought iron registers covered large holes in the floors. Mom said the furnace in the cellar would send heat up through those iron registers and hopefully warm us to our bones.

But presently we shivered as the cold rooms seemed to cry out for heat. The walls creaked with every move and the windows rattled with the fierce winds that moaned and groaned against the thin walls.

Mom looked to Glen again and her sad eyes became sadder.

"Come upstairs, everybody!" Dad now called from the top of the staircase. "Let me show you where you kids will be sleepin'."

At the top of the stairs we gathered in a spacious room lightened by four large windows that rattled recklessly with the bitter winds. Dad felt along the windowsill and the sharp winds nipped at his fingers. "I guess we'll need t' seal these windows with some tape. If we don't, we'll have more cold air comin' into this house than heat, that's for sure."

Dad inspected the other windows and his face told us they, too, needed tape. Finally, he spoke again. "We'll keep all you boys in this room an' the girls in the small room next t' it," he explained as he nodded his head in the direction of a much smaller room sitting at the front of the house. "This way we can block those larger rooms, in the back, an' keep what little heat there will be confined t' your bedrooms."

"What heat, Dad? I don't see any registers up here," Roberta said and then shivered at the thought.

"Well, I warned you it's gonna be mighty cold up here. I'm afraid the only heat you're gonna get is from your blankets an' your own body heat, girls. However, we'll leave the door at the bottom of the stairs open an' some heat will come up through it."

"Hey, everybody, come an' see this!" Henry called from the girls' tiny bedroom. "Jist look at that scenery out there!" He leaned against the west window and stared in awe.

Crowding around the window we all gazed out upon acres and acres of snow-covered maple trees, pine trees, oak trees, and apple trees. As far as our eyes could see there were trees. To the left, among those trees we could see traces of Anglin' Road as it bobbed along the rolling hills. It dipped here and there and hid behind the trees and then rose again on some small knoll. In the far distance, a lonely house curled its thick, gray smoke above the horizon as it nestled unseen in the woods beyond.

"Beautiful, ain't it, kids!" Dad rested his strong arm on Henry's shoulder and peered across the white earth below. "I swear this can be some place if we want it t' be! There're lots of possibilities here." With those words, Dad backed away from the window. "I think we've had enough fun for awhile," he said. "It's time t' get busy an' get this place ready t' live in."

As Dad, Henry, and Robert set up the beds and arranged the dressers, Esther, Roberta and we smaller boys carried blankets and pillows upstairs.

By late evening we were ten tired souls, exhausted and anxious to crawl into bed in our new sleeping quarters. In one hand Dad carefully carried the soft, flickering lamp up the stairs and led us to our respective rooms. In the other hand he held a strange, large, blue bucket with a lid on top and set it beside the banister between the girls' bedroom and the boys' bedroom. "This is your bathroom," he told us. He smiled now as he set the large, blue bucket on the floor. "We'll put the lamp right here on this dresser," he said as he set the kerosene lamp gently between the two bedrooms. "There will be plenty of light for both rooms. Just be careful! An' don't fool around or this lamp could be tipped over very easily!"

5 | Henry's Frightening Ghost Story

Three beds were set up in the boys' bedroom. In the first bed, to the north wall, Robert and I jumped quickly under the fluffy blankets and nestled comfortably in. In the far corner of our bedroom, Eddie and Wesley leaped into their long rope bed and quickly hid beneath three thick blankets.

"I'm freezin'!" Wesley shouted through shivering teeth.

"You're not the only one freezin'," Eddie said. "It must be zero degrees outside."

"Outside?" I said. "I think it's zero degrees inside."

"It's no warmer in this room, I assure you," Roberta called from the girls' bedroom.

"In fact, you guys get the warm air coming up the stairs. We get nothing in here!" Esther said.

"What are you babies cryin' 'bout? This is invigoratin'! It's good for ya!" Henry shivered the words through the dark room. In an isolated cot, between the other two beds, he curled his lanky body into a warm ball and sank with the weak springs until the thin, quilted mattress wrapped around his loins and locked him in.

Esther, in her long, faded nightgown, scurried her naked feet across the wintry floor and blew across the kerosene lamp, snuffing its golden flames. Then, quickly, she whisked back to the tiny bedroom where she snuggled tightly against Roberta in their stately, brass bed.

When the light from the kerosene lamp suddenly went out our eyes became useless in the strange, cold room. That's when Henry started again. "It sure is dark up here—*ain't it, you guys?*" Henry called across the pitch-black rooms. "Kinda scary in fact, *ain't it?*"

"I hadn't thought much 'bout it," I announced, hoping to build confidence in my voice. But somehow the night air and the gloomy atmosphere of our room only seemed to verify Henry's haunting words.

"I've seen darker nights," Robert declared. "You're just tryin' t' scare us, that's all."

"Well, I wasn't gonna tell ya 'bout that noise in the other room, but maybe it's for your own good that ya know."

"What noise?" Eddie blurted out as he sprang up in his bed.

"Oh, 'twasn't nothin', prob'ly. Ghosts don't come out this early anyways."

"Who said anythin' 'bout ghosts?" Robert complained.

As though he had not heard Robert's question, Henry asked, "Have ya guys been in the other rooms next t' our bedroom, yet?"

"Of course we have! And there's nothing in there either," Esther said from under her covers. Three long, curly locks dangled loosely above the covers. Quickly, Esther snatched them from the crisp air and tucked them safely under the blankets.

"Oh, I know ya didn't see nothin' t'day. But ya gotta admit, it's a perfect place for a body t' hide at night time!"

"A body?" Eddie blurted out. "You mean a *dead* body?"

"Sure, I mean a *body! A dead b-o-d-y-y-y!*" Henry said, dragging the word body with such a frightening voice. "Which reminds me, did I ever tell ya 'bout the little boy who was sent t' the butcher's t' buy some liver?"

Outside, the winds howled louder. The rain gutter slapped against the siding of the house and the windows shook and sang haunting songs.

"Well," Henry continued, "the butcher told the little boy there wasn't no liver left. *But!* If he went t' the graveyard he could get some liver from 'mong the tombstones. It seems every night the graveyard keeper would put some fresh liver out for the graveyard ghosts who came out every night t' eat. This kept the ghosts happy and thereby friendly with everyone."

"That's good!" I cried softly, deep under my covers.

"But *nobody* would dare take this liver 'cause it was owned by the ghosts of the graveyard. And *nobody* wanted t' anger the ghosts of the graveyard!"

"Of course not!" I shivered the words past my trembling lips.

"It sure is dark in here," Eddie interrupted.

"Well, the boy was brave," Henry continued, "an' he went t' the graveyard that night and *stole the liver from the graveyard!*"

"Oh, no!" I gasped, shaking in my bed.

"Well, he brought it home and his mother *cooked it!*"

"Oh, no! She shouldn' hab don' dat!" Wesley gulped.

"*Well, she did!*" Henry continued. "And it tasted good! However, after supper his mother found out 'bout where he got that liver and she sent him straight t' bed! His bedroom, by the way, was like ours—*just like ours!*" Then with a voice that surely came from the graveyard, Henry said, *"Dark! cold and s-p-o-o-k-y!"*

"Go on! Go on!" Robert said, staring through the pitch dark of the night. "Let's git this over with!"

"Well," Henry continued again, "he fell asleep only t' wake up late at night with a full moon shinin' through his bedroom window."

I lifted the covers from my head and bravely glanced to the foot of our bed. The pale moon had broken through the dark clouds and now lay frozen at the foot of our beds.

"At first, everythin' was still... and... quiet.... Then he heard somethin'... !" Henry continued. Slowly now, in dead silence,

Henry slipped the covers from his warm body. Crawling on his stomach and elbows he slowly inched quietly to the top of the stairs. *"It was somebody comin' up his bedroom steps… !"* Henry called as his frightening voice echoed across the somber walls.

"I'm not going to listen to anymore of this nonsense," Esther objected as she poked her index fingers into her ears and buried her head firmly under her goose-down pillow. "I wish we would have stayed in Brookfield!"

"I'm the ghost of the graveyard!" Henry bellowed with the most terrifying, quivering voice we had ever heard. *"I came t' get my liver!"* the voice said. *"I'm on your first step! Thump!"* Henry paused while the cold winds screamed at the bedroom windows. *"Now I'm on your second step!"* The ghost of the graveyard continued. *"I came t' get my liver! Thump!"*

"How many steps do we hab, Eddie?" Wesley whispered through chattering teeth.

"Th - th - th - ir - teen, Wesley! I counted th - th - them with Henry t'day."

Slowly now, Henry continued to drag the ghost of the graveyard through each of the terrible, thirteen steps and '*Thumps*' until, finally, he reached our bedroom. While our heads were still covered and our beds were shaking so much we feared the rattling would wake the remaining ghosts of the graveyard, Henry crept ever so quietly on hands and knees through the dark, dreary room. Then, with a voice that quivered and shook, Henry cried, *"I'm in your room and I want my liver!"*

Suddenly, with a leap and a bound, Henry sprang from the floor and plunged head first into bed with Robert and me screaming, *"I got ya!"*

"E-e-e-e-e-!" Everybody cried out at Henry's merciless act.

From the girls' bedroom, muffled moans chattered across the air. Brother Wesley cried while Eddie gasped for air. But in our bed, Robert and I lay stiff and white, victims of the ghost of the graveyard.

Finally, Henry crawled clumsily from our bed and screamed across the night air until every rafter shook and seemed certain to tumble to the floor below.

"Quiet down up there or I'll bring a stick up!" Mom shouted from the foot of the stairs. "We've got a lot of work to do around here tomorrow and you'll need your sleep! Now get to sleep this instant! And I mean it!"

"How's a person s'posta get t' sleep when they keep screamin' up here?" Henry pleaded innocently then snickered loudly under his covers.

But we were too frightened to tell the truth about Henry scaring us with his frightening ghost story. Besides, if we did, we feared Henry might jump on us again the next night. So not a word was said in our defense.

As the frightening moments wore on, we finally did settle down. But not until Henry fell asleep did I dare close my eyes. Once I was sure Henry was fast asleep, I sighed a big sigh of relief, slipped my head out of the covers, and slowly scanned the room to see if any of Henry's ghosts were left over from his dreadful story. But sometimes, throughout the long night, I could hear a creak or two from one of the other rooms. I wondered if perhaps there really was someone, or some thing, hiding in there, just waiting for the precise moment to jump out and grab one of us from our dark bedrooms.

6 | The Singing School Bus

Monday morning came and our thoughts were on school. It was a bright morning. The sun had broken through the dismal clouds and now its golden rays were penetrating the near translucent windows, reaching into the darkest corners, hurrying the night shadows away. But they were cold rays; rays that seemed to prick one's flesh like a thousand icy needles. Hurriedly we donned our winter clothes and quickly we scampered down the cold, hollow stairs to gather ourselves around the large kitchen table.

In the cellar, Dad stoked the furnace. He poked the golden ambers of the dying flames with a long, iron rod. Watching the colorful sparks dance and come to life, he then shoveled one more shovel full of bituminous coal upon the yellow flames, set the damper, and finally climbed the cellar steps.

Mom stood at the wood stove mixing scrambled eggs and fried potatoes. "You kids behave at school today now. Do you hear me?" She leaned across the kitchen table and scraped the eggs and potatoes into a large bowl. "I don't want to hear any bad words about any of you now." Turning back to the stove she began mixing another batch of eggs and potatoes. "And Carl, you make sure you put cotton in those ears of yours and pull that stocking cap down over your ears."

"Yes, Mom," I said as I quickly downed the eggs and potatoes on my plate.

When each of us finished eating, we took turns at the kitchen sink splashing ice cold water on our faces then drying and combing our hair in front of the mirror that hung directly above the tin water bucket. As we put our winter coats and boots on Mom pointed to six lunches, each wrapped in a section of the latest newspaper and tied with string. "Don't forget your lunches," she said and then scooted us out the door. From the kitchen window she, Dad, Glen, and Wesley waved goodbye.

On a small knoll, Roberta perched herself high above the rest of us, peering the distant hills, eagerly anticipating the first sign of the yellow school bus. "Here it comes, you guys! The bus is coming!" She called as her spreading arms glided her quickly down the slippery, snow-covered road. Her red knitted scarf flapped in the wild breeze and cold tears rushed past her temples.

It was a peculiar looking school bus. I had never seen one like it before. Our bus in Brookfield was long and had about thirty seats in it. Each seat was behind another. But this bus was different. Although it was yellow and looked exactly like the larger buses at Brookfield, it was much smaller. There were two long seats running from the front of the bus to the rear with their backs to each other. Then, strange as it may seem, there were two long seats running along each side of the bus, facing the two seats, which ran down the middle. The seat on the left was broken and just lying on the floor of the bus. Two young girls squatted on the broken seat while throughout the tiny bus, seven or eight other children watched with hawk-like eyes as we tread our way down the narrow aisle.

"Would you like to have this seat?" A smiling girl motioned to Esther as she, Roberta, and I stepped to the middle of the bus. The friendly girl lifted a stack of books from a vacant seat and gestured with her free hand to the empty seat. Two coal-black braids hung from each side of the girl's head and rested in frayed ends upon her thin shoulders. She smiled again and as her eyes twinkled; her gapped teeth sparkled like a freshly painted fence.

"Thank you, but I'll sit down here on the broken seat with my brother and sister," Esther answered with a returned smile, plopping herself to the floor of the bus.

"This must be the girls' side of the bus," I whispered to Esther. "All the girls are over here! And all the boys are over there!"

"Well, why don't you go over there then?" Roberta whispered back, smiling to the girls around her.

"What's your name?" the girl with the coal-black braids asked.

"Esther. This is my brother, Carl. I guess he's a little scared," Esther replied.

"I'm Roberta," Roberta quickly offered.

"What grade are you in?" The same girl spoke again, directing her question to me. I refused to answer.

"He's in second grade," Esther said, coming to my rescue. "I'm in the sixth grade and Roberta's in the fifth grade."

"He's a cute kid," the girl said to Esther. "A little bashful though, isn't he? I'm Elizabeth Williamson. You can call me Liz, though. All my friends do. This is Barb and Florence Wilson, and that's Ruth Hoffman sitting there beside you. You'll like it here at Hartford—specially on the bus. We have a lot of fun."

As the small, yellow bus slowly crossed over the wooden bridge, near our house, the bus driver yelled, "Watch out!" And then he slammed on the brakes.

"Look to the front of the bus, everybody!" He called with excitement in his voice. Directly in front of us a large herd of deer seemed to glide across Anglin' Road as though they were on a large carousel.

"Twelve deer!" Someone yelled. "There are twelve of them today!"

"I'll bet they're no more than twenty feet in front of us," the bus driver said.

Never before had I been so close to such a beautiful animal! Never before had I been held so spellbound! Of course I recalled the deer I had seen the other day, but they were so far away! These deer were so close I could reach out and touch them!

"Beautiful, aren't they!" Liz said. "There's lots of deer around here. We see them quite often like this."

"We saw about six deer on our way here the other day," Esther began as she lowered herself to her seat. "But they were much farther away. I just love deer! When I saw those deer the other day, I thought I would never live to see such a sight again."

"Well, believe me, I wouldn't be surprised if we have to stop like this a dozen or more times before school's out in May," Barb said. "They run in herds like that all the time." She pulled her round, wire-rimmed glasses from the bridge of her nose, puffed across the top, and with a circular motion of her wrist quickly wiped them clean. Then she continued. "Dad puts a salt lick behind our barn just to lure them near. Then he sets corn out in the fields and we watch them come and eat!"

Barb was a pretty girl. At first she had appeared old and not so attractive to me. But now, behind the glasses, I could see that she was very young, perhaps Esther's age, and most attractive with her narrow chin and broad smile that formed two, deep depressions at each end.

"Hey, Liz," the girl named Ruth shouted when all had become quiet. "What are you and Ronny gonna sing this morning?"

Though she was somewhat heavy for a young girl, Ruth was not fat. She was what Dad would have called 'stocky', a good farm girl. When she opened her mouth she displayed two badly decayed teeth. But her smile was warm and pleasant, and in spite of myself, I, at last, had discovered that I, too, was smiling.

"They sing every day on our bus," Barb said to Esther. "You just gotta hear them! They're really good!"

"Come on, Liz!" Ruth begged.

"Yeah! Come on, Liz! Let's hear you and Ronny sing before we get to school," the others chanted.

"Are you ready, Ronny?" Liz called as she turned and faced the boys' side of the bus.

"Sure! I've been ready! I'm just waiting for you," a small dark haired boy replied from the other side of the bus. He rose from his seat and while the tiny bus bobbed and swayed Ronny inched his way to the rear of the bus.

Ronny was small, not much taller than me. But the girls said he was really in the fifth grade which made him Robert's and Roberta's age. His hair was pitch-black and his eyes a deep, dark brown.

"His parents are from Spain," Barb whispered to Esther. "His last name is Santana. He lives just up the road from you. You couldn't see his house because of all the trees, but he lives on the next road west of your house. Just wait till you hear him sing! He's got the most beautiful voice you'll ever hear!"

I gazed intently now as Liz bent her long, slender body and reached under the lengthy seat. Soon, her fingers latched securely around a long handle and I waited anxiously to see just what it could be. Now, as the girls' legs parted to allow more room, I could plainly see that the long handle was part of a small, brown guitar. Strapping the guitar around her neck, Liz carefully edged her way to the rear of the bus where she and Ronny now stood and smiled to the excited onlookers. Then, all became unusually quiet as Liz began to chord her small guitar. Softly now, as the voice of an angel, Ronny began to sing:

"When they begin the Beguine
It brings back the sound of music so

tender,
It brings back a night of tropical splendor
It brings back a memory ever green.
I'm with you once more under the stars
And down by the shore an orchestra's
playing
Even the palms seem to be swaying,
When they begin the Beguine…"

How beautiful Ronny's voice was! Never before had I heard such a strong and exquisite voice coming from such a young boy! How splendid Liz was as her nimble fingers flew across the strings of her guitar!

"Let's sing, 'Ole Buttermilk Sky', Ronny," Liz said as they finished singing the first song. Immediately, her fingers stroked the mellow guitar and she began to sing as Ronny began to harmonize:

"Ole buttermilk sky,
I'm keepin' my eye peeled on you,
What's the good word tonight?
Are you gonna be mellow tonight?
Ole buttermilk sky,
Can't you see my little donkey and me?
We're as happy as a Christmas tree,
Headin' for the one I love.
I'm gonna pop her the question, that question,
Do you Darlin', do you do?
It'll be easy, so easy,
If I can only bank on you.
Ole buttermilk sky
I'm a tellin' you why, now you know,

Keep it in mind tonight,
Ole buttermilk sky,
Don't you tell me when I'm needin' you most,
Hang a moon above her hitchin' post,
Hitch me to the one I love.
You can if you try,
Don't tell me no lie,
Will you be mellow and bright tonight?
Ole buttermilk sky."

For the first time, I now felt completely comfortable as my very bones seemed to dance for joy. Henry, Robert, and Eddie joined in and clapped to the rhythm of the song. Esther and Roberta sang along. Even the bus driver kept time to the music as his foot thumped the hard floorboard and his fingers tapped the steering wheel. Music filled the air and happiness settled deep in my soul. I thought of Glen and how he had taught himself to chord a small ukulele and how he and Esther and Roberta sang just like this at home. How I wished that Glen could be here! How beautiful his deep baritone voice would blend in with Ronny's high, tenor tones. They were good thoughts now. But now we were at school and that presented another problem.

7 | "You're Too Small to be in School!"

There was nothing unusual about Hartford Centralized School. It was small, though it possessed two floors and a basement. It was built of light brown brick, had a miniature gymnasium, twelve classrooms (one for each of the twelve grades), a very small library, a principal's office, and a miniature kitchen. The strange thing was— the school sat right in the middle of a road! The bus driver told Roberta that years ago the small, one-room schoolhouse used to sit to the south of the road, but one night it caught fire and burned to the ground. The citizens of Hartford voted to build a new and better school and for some unknown reason chose to move the site to its present location and there it still remained.

"That's the second-grade room on the left," Barb said as Esther, Barb, and I climbed the steps to the main floor. "You'll be in my room, Esther. We're on the second floor. Mrs. Hamilton is our teacher. She's mean, but we all like her." Barb continued up the next flight of steps alone and paused at the first landing.

"This is your room, Carl," Esther said and then shoved me to the door. "I've got to go to my room now, so you just go in and tell the teacher who you are. I'll see you after school."

In a moment, Esther skipped up the next flight of steps where she met Barb and soon the two of them vanished from view as I stood alone in the long corridor. Down the hallway, I could see Eddie as he entered his room with another young boy he had met on the school bus. Henry and Robert had gone ahead to their room with Ronny Santana as their guide, while Roberta trailed behind.

Slowly, I reached to the doorknob and pulled the heavy wooden door open. At the front of the room, the hatchet-faced teacher was presently examining the bruised elbow of a wailing, tow-headed boy and did not notice, nor seem to care, that I had entered the room. But just like wildfire, the news of a strange, new face had reached every ear in the room and soon the entire class was searching me with piercing eyes.

Frightened, I took a deep breath hoping to settle my rapid heartbeats. I knew I must have looked silly wearing Eddie's old coat. But that's the way it was. I outgrew my coat and Mom told me to wear Eddie's coat because he outgrew his. He was now wearing Robert's old coat and Robert was wearing Henry's old coat. But Eddie's coat was much too big for me.

Now, as I stood at the rear of the room, my coat collar was turned up high resembling two horse blinders. My scarf draped over my right shoulder, nearly touching the floor. My stocking cap hung over both ears, partially covering my eyes.

Suddenly, my nose began to drip and quickly I zipped my clean, white handkerchief from the long coat sleeve, wiped my runny nose and hid the handkerchief back in the sleeve.

"That was funny!" A redheaded, freckled face girl in the back row said. She held her hand to her smiling lips and softly whispered, "Do that again!"

Now, the teacher was aware of my presence as the class began to snicker. "And just who are you, little boy?" she asked as she rose from her chair and walked to the back of the room where I stood, scanning the strange faces that now stared back at me.

"I'm Carl," I somehow managed to say.

The teacher had a pleasant smile, but the closer she came the more frightened I became. Large brown circles completely covered her long dress. A strong smell of fresh gardenia perfume nearly made me dizzy. As she stood beside me I suddenly realized she was extremely tall and 'thin as a stick', as Dad would have said.

"Well, Carl, what brings you here today?"

"The school bus," I said.

The class began to chuckle.

The teacher smiled too, holding back her own laughter. "I know the school bus brought you here, but *why* is what I'd like to know." She began to laugh, now. "*You're too small to be in school!*"

Before I could stop her, the teacher reached down and gently lifted my stocking cap from my perspiring head. As the cap rose from my head it latched on to the pieces of cotton I had poked in each ear and instantly they dropped to the floor.

Now the class began to laugh louder.

I stooped to pick the cotton balls up and hastily I poked them back into my ears. 'Too small for school? What did she mean by that?' I wondered. 'You must have t' be a certain height before they let ya in school!'

"You can't be in second grade! You're too small! You must be in first grade." This time she spoke with authority.

'First grade? That's funny!' I thought again. 'I was tall enough t' be in the second grade at Brookfield.'

"Do you have any brothers or sisters here?" She continued to question me while still holding my stocking cap.

"Yes," I answered.

"What grades are they in, Carl?" Now she held my hand in hers and gently patted it, much like a pampering mother. My face became hot with embarrassment.

"My brother, Eddie's in the third grade an' Esther's in the sixth grade, an' Roberta, Henry an' Robert are in the fifth grade. An' Glen and Wesley are at home." And then I remembered Darlene.

"An' I have a cousin in second grade in Brookfield—*an' she's the same size I am!*" I proudly replied.

"Okay," the teacher said. Holding her one hand to her smiling lips, she briskly rubbed my head with the other. "I'll go ask your sister in the sixth grade which grade you're really in."

Turning to the class, she exclaimed, "Now class, you behave while I'm gone. I won't be but a minute."

Though in front of me nearly forty eyes continued to twinkle and laugh at me, I felt all alone at the rear of the room. Then a chubby, blonde boy called across the room to a much taller boy sitting near the front of the room. "Hey, Herb!" he shouted boldly, with his hand cupped around his mouth. "I'll bet you're afraid to do it now!"

"No, I'm not!" Herb returned with a bit of anger in his voice.

It was quite obvious that whatever the task was that now lay ahead of Herb, it had been planned for some time to be put into operation at such an opportune time as this.

"Yes, you are, scaredy-cat!"

"No, I'm not!" This time Herb's body stiffened with anger while his red eyes flashed bitterly.

"Yes, you are!" The blonde haired boy spoke calmly now, as though he was prepared to continue this chant until doomsday. "You're nothing more than a scaredy-cat!"

"I'm not a scaredy-cat and don't you call me that again!"

"If you're not a scaredy-cat why don't you do it then—scaredy-cat!"

" 'Cause he's afraid to. That's why he won't do it." But this time the voice came from a girl with a deep voice who almost looked albino. She jabbed Herb with her sharp pencil from behind.

"Herb is a scaredy-cat! Herb is a scaredy-cat!" The entire class began to chant now.

At the rear of the room, I continued to stand alone, somewhat relieved that the attention was now focused on a young boy named Herb. Now, I waited also, to see just how Herb would handle the problem now confronting him.

At first Herb's face seemed pale, almost sickly. Then his face became bright red just like the red shirt he wore. His clenched fists gripped his desk and became white at the knuckles. He grit his teeth and his lips curled like an angry tiger.

Suddenly, as if he were tempted beyond control, Herb bolted from his chair with his books, pencils, and papers under his arms and shot like a house afire to the nearest window. From the front corner of the room, he snatched a long, slender pole with an iron hook at the end used for pulling the upper windows down. Thrusting it under the lower window he gave a hearty push and up flew the window. Now, while the wintry winds howled and blew across the room, Herb angrily hurled his personal belongings out the window, watching them flutter up and over like feathers in a wild, blustery windstorm.

For a moment total silence filled the room. Then, as if by instruction, the entire class broke into a round of applause and mischievous titters and giggles once again filled the room as Herb returned triumphantly to his seat. As he approached his desk, Herb tipped his head as a sovereign king and proudly accepted the royalty he so well deserved.

At that moment the teacher returned to the room. There was no laughter now. The only sound was that of little fingers sifting the pages of textbooks and a broken cough or two, a perfect semblance of a well disciplined class.

"Well, Carl, you're in second grade all right," the teacher said as she rested her hands on her narrow hips.

How relieved I was to hear those words! I was tall enough to be in the second grade after all!

8 | Herb Fights Back

Quickly, I unbuckled my boots, kicked them into the long closet, and hastily hung my coat on a spare hanger. Now I waited as the teacher spoke. "Since there are no more desks available," she said, "somebody will have to share his desk with Carl."

Before she could say anymore, each of the boys and two girls raised their hands.

Instantly, a large, plump girl slid to the side of her seat and quickly brushed the remainder of her seat with her right hand as she waved her left hand vigorously.

"Oh, no!" I whispered under my breath. "Please don't make me sit there!"

"Thank you for your thoughtfulness, Debbie," the teacher said quickly and politely. "But I think we'd better let Carl sit with a boy. I think he might feel a little more comfortable that way."

Then, for some unknown reason, the teacher turned to Herb and said, "Thank you, Herb. That's very nice of you to share your desk with Carl. Now hurry along, Carl." She smiled as she nudged me toward Herb's desk.

Once again soft giggles filled the once hushed room.

"By the way, Herb," the teacher added, "you will have to share your books, too. We'll get some books for you later, Carl."

In the twinkling of an eye, the once suppressed giggles turned to an outburst of laughter and the shrill voice of the short, chubby, blonde boy rang throughout the room as he blurted out excitedly,

"Herb doesn't have any books to share, Mrs. Dilly! He threw them out the window!"

"He what?" she cried out as she whirled around. Her eyes turned to red saucers.

"That's right, Mrs. Dilly! He just got up and threw them out that window, over there!" The girl with the deep voice pointed to the large window at the front of the room.

"Oh, he did, did he?"

And now her eyes flashed with fire as she approached the large window. There, on the cold white ground below, Herb's papers swirled with the blustery whirlwinds. Three wet books flapped briskly in the wild breeze.

Bewildered, Mrs. Dilly stared first at the books and papers swirling and flapping in the cold wind and then at Herb who sat sheepishly at our desk. Then, as if beyond control of her normal thinking, Mrs. Dilly darted suddenly to our desk with flames growing wildly in each eye. *"You just come here, young man!"* She reached across me and latched firmly to the back of Herb's neck.

But Herb was not about to leave his only protection as he clung tightly to his desk and grit his teeth once again.

"Young man, I command you to let go of that desk and come here this instant! Do you hear me?" she yelled.

As in Brookfield, each desk was made of wood and bolted to the floor with metal legs. Herb wrapped his legs around the metal legs and gripped tighter to his desk.

"Come here, I said!"

But the harder she pulled the tighter Herb clung to his desk.

First, Mrs. Dilly pulled Herb over me until I almost slid off the seat and to the floor. Then, just as quickly, Herb pulled her over me and nearly smothered me. Herb was over me and then Mrs. Dilly was over me, then Herb, then Mrs. Dilly once again.

Finally, Mrs. Dilly stopped pulling and stood beside our desk with her hands on her hips. "Would you please move your little body, Carl?"

Gratefully, I jumped from the desk while around me the laughter rose higher and higher.

Desperate now, Mrs. Dilly reached down and grasped her thin fingers firmly around Herb's ankles. Immediately, Herb's body stretched across the aisle, stiff as an ironing board. But Herb clung tightly to his desk.

"Do ya want me t' help ya, Mrs. Dilly?" I asked.

"No thank you, Carl. Just stay out of the way! I'll do all right without your help."

But the harder she pulled and tugged the louder Herb hollered and screamed. Now it just seemed hopeless to me. She would never get Herb to give in. She would never win this battle unless I came to her aid. Quickly, I latched on to Herb's waist and joined the pulling contest. First, Herb's body went this way - and then that way - until it seemed it should have snapped. But it did not snap. And the class cheered on. There seemed to be no end to Herb's persistence.

But finally Herb's exhausted body became weak. Defeated, his fingers slipped from the desk and his loose body bounced into Mrs. Dilly's determined arms. Whack! Whack! Whack! The hard, wooden ruler echoed across the room.

"Serves him right," said the girl with the deep voice as Herb's screams bounced off the walls. "He's a bad little boy!"

"Thank you for your assistance, Carl. But the next time I tell you I don't need your help, that's exactly what I mean! *And as for you, young man,*" directing her anger to Herb, Mrs. Dilly said, *"you get your little body out that door and pick those books and papers up! And I mean right now!"*

When our tiny school bus dropped us off at our driveway that day, Aunt Rose stood in the front lawn. Her arms reached out to hug each of us. "I've missed you little heathens more than you can ever guess," she said. Her eyes became misty.

We gathered around Aunt Rose and followed her to the house. At the door, Uncle Clyde began to laugh in his silly way. "My, my, my!" he said. Then he hugged each of us. He just stood there and laughed. Then he pulled his pants up with his wrists.

What fun it was as we gathered around the long kitchen table at the end of that first school day, sharing the events of the day! Roberta told of the funny little school bus while Robert raved of Ronny's and Liz's singing. Esther described each of her new friends, and when Mom left the table to put the butter into the icebox, Henry whispered how he and Ronny made plans for playing hooky on their birthdays, which happened to fall on the same day in February.

"Henry's gonna play hooky," Wesley said while we all snickered and looked to one another in surprise.

Mom turned around and returned to the table. "What's this about hooky?" she asked with a puzzled look on her face. Aunt Rose gave a long scowl. Uncle Clyde snickered.

"Oh, Wesley can't hear well, Mom. I was jist tellin' everybody that one of my classmates said his dad was a bookie."

Henry stared at Wesley with a mean look and Wesley said, "You said, 'hooky'."

That's when I spoke up and told of my dreadful experience of nearly being too small for school and finished with the wild antics of a boy named Herb.

But it was Eddie who drew the loudest laughter as he unfolded the long and amusing story of the heavy-set girl who was sent to the rear of the room for being bad. "She got tired of standin' there," he snickered. "So she sat down in the wastebasket. And wouldn't ya know it! She got stuck!"

"What did she do then?" Glen asked as delightful tears rolled down his cheeks.

"Billy Johnson, my new friend, who lives jist up the road an' rides our bus, suggested we get a crowbar and pry her out!"

"Show's good thinkin' if ya ask me," Henry said as joyful faces continued to laugh.

"Then one of the girls said we should go down an' get some butter and spread it all over her, and then we could just slide her out!" Eddie continued.

"What did you finally do?" Mom asked with a chuckle in her voice.

"The teacher finally sent someone down t' get the janitor. He pulled on the wastebasket an' the teacher pulled on the girl an' she finally popped out."

It was so good to see Aunt Rose and Uncle Clyde again.

As we lay in bed that evening, we told and retold the events of the day. As the lazy minutes ticked away and our hearts sang with laughter, we soon exhausted ourselves. Gradually, we drifted into a pleasant sleep.

9 | "A Woman's Been Murdered in Our Woods!"

I awoke to the sound of a distant train as it rumbled across the trestle expanding Anglin' Road. Until we had moved to Anglin' Road, I had never known the wondrous sound of the train whistle. The blast of a far-a-way train whistle, the chug, chug, chug, as the train grinds away up a small knoll, and the click, click, click as it rolls over the iron tracks were the most beautiful sounds I had ever heard. I recalled Uncle Slim telling me the sound of a train whistle was nearly as beautiful as the sounds of nature itself. No one could deny the beauty of an ocean wave rolling gently across the silvery sands of a warm beach, or a mother bird calling to her loved ones, or the wintry winds howling through the tall pines. But Uncle Slim said more songs had been written about train whistles than any other sound created by man. It was a foreign sound—a sound that lulled babies and grown-ups to sleep—a sound that set a grown man to wishing he were a child again—a sound that brought tears to a mother's eyes, dreaming of far-a-way places with strange sounding names. It was a sound of wanting—meeting—going—returning—loneliness—and love—all in one.

Now, as I lay in bed, the wonderful sounds of that train whistle whirled around in my head almost making me dizzy with delight. Then I heard Dad's voice booming from the bottom of the bedroom stairs. "You boys get up now. I got somethin' t' show you."

Quickly, we slipped our clothes on and rambled down the stairs. Dad led us outside to the shanty on the far side of the driveway. Reaching into the shanty, he pulled out some strange metal devices with short chains attached. Holding them in front of us all, he said, "This isn't for all you boys, but I want you all t' pay close attention t' what I have t' say."

Then he looked directly at Henry and Robert. "Maybe this will keep you two out of trouble," he said. "Besides that, you both are old enough t' start earnin' some good income." Then he looked very seriously at Henry and Robert. "Do you know what these are?" he asked.

"They're animal traps of some kind," Henry spoke up.

"You're absolutely right, Henry. They're muskrat traps. Muskrat pelts are bringin' two t' four dollars a piece, dependin' on the size an' quality of the fur. I'll teach you boys how t' set these traps, skin the muskrats, an' stretch their hides. Then it's up t' you."

Dad then dropped one of the traps to the ground, stepped on its spring and the jaws of the trap opened wide. He set the lock on the foot plate and released the spring with his foot. The trap was now set. Reaching to the ground, he picked up a stick about the size of a muskrat's leg and carefully set it on the foot plate. Before we could blink our eyes the trap sprung loose and clamped its powerful jaws around that stick and snapped it to pieces. "That's what will happen t' your fingers if you dare get them caught," he warned them. "Safety must be foremost in your minds. Never get so cocky that you forget it or you'll lose a finger quicker than a snake's tongue!" He looked seriously to Henry and Robert. "Did you hear me, boys?"

"Yes, Dad. We got the message all right!" Robert said.

That evening Henry and Robert decided to set their traps along Yankee Creek. The bitter, westerly winds howled through the quaking aspen trees as they made their way along Yankee Creek. Crusted snow beneath their feet crunched like potato chips warning wild animals they were near. On the opposite side of the creek a large doe paused, still as a statue, and then she quickly darted into the nearby thicket.

New snow began to cover the old snow and fresh muskrat tracks led to large holes along the banks of Yankee Creek. Henry chipped the thick ice above the muskrat holes with a large branch he found along the bank. Carefully, he slid the trap in front of the entrance to the hole. A long chain led to a metal ring at the end. Robert drove a t-shaped stick through this ring and pounded it deep into the frozen ground. In the same fashion, each of the other traps was set. Now they would wait until the next morning to check their traps.

On the way home the snow had stopped falling. Occasionally the silver moon broke through the gray clouds. Robert stopped and stared into a large, dense section of woods across Yankee Creek. "Someday I'm gonna walk through those woods an' see that place they call Lovers' Lane," he said more to himself than to Henry.

"I wouldn't git too many ideas in my head if I was you, young man. Ya know what Mom has said since she heard about that place. She must have told us t' stay away from there at least a hundred times."

"I know," Robert said. "It's a bad place. She and Aunt Rose keep tellin' us it's a place where boys an' girls go t' kiss. But I heard it's also a beautiful place t' see in any season. I just want t' see for myself, that's all."

"Well, whatever ya do, don't let Mom or Aunt Rose know you've been thinkin' 'bout it. We'll all hear that sermon again about only bad people go there."

"I know," Robert said, and the conversation was ended.

Every morning Henry and Robert rose before the sun and set out to check their traps. When the sun set in the evening, they set out again. Often, there were two or three muskrats in their burlap sacks when they returned. Before they went to bed they skinned the hides from the muskrats and stretched their warm furs on flat boards that looked like miniature ironing boards. In the cold, winter air, hot steam rose from the hides and gave off a strong stench of death. In a few days the skins were dried and Henry and Robert took them to Mr. Parker in Hartford Center.

Mr. Parker stood in a rundown add-on to his house. Dried pelts hung across each wall and dead muskrats lay on the floor. Tools and furniture that would never be used again crammed the walls. The sickening stench of dead animals filled the room and Robert's stomach began to turn. He held his breath, but when at long last he let out a gasp to breathe again, a larger breath of stale air was sucked in and the horrible smell went deep into his stomach and began to stir.

Two matted cats sniffed the dead muskrats lying on the floor. Displeased with the smell, they left to begin their search for mice.

Bearing a strong resemblance to Johnny Appleseed, Mr. Parker plopped Henry's and Robert's pelts down on his makeshift counter. His long, straggly beard looked as though it had never been brushed, reminding Henry and Robert of an old, used mop.

"Seems t' me this one must have been in a fight. Looks like he lost some of his fur," he said as he held the muskrat's pelt by its hind legs and pulled at its fur. He chewed hard on a large wad of tobacco and then spit on the floor. Then he continued. "Not worth more than a dollar at the most. But I still have that Christmas spirit, so I'll give you two dollars, boys."

There was no debating the price. Mr. Parker was firm and mean. But Henry and Robert were excited to see the dollar bills drop into their hands. For the first time in their lives they were working, enjoying it, and making a profit.

Sometimes Mr. Parker said the pelts were too small. Other times he said they were too old. Each time he handed Henry and Robert no more than two dollars for each pelt. Once, Henry became extra brave and questioned Mr. Parker. "Seems t' me this pelt's worth more than two dollars," he declared boldly. "Just look at that fur! You won't find a nicer pelt than that this side of the Allegheny Mountains."

Robert, surprised at Henry's new boldness and his sudden knowledge of muskrats this side of the Allegheny Mountains looked first to Henry and then to Mr. Parker.

Mr. Parker looked up from the muskrat pelt that lay on the counter. His dark brown eyes began to flare. He stared Henry in the eye and chewed harder on his tobacco. Then, before Henry knew what to think, Mr. Parker spit a large wad of tobacco past Henry's ear, wiped his lips with the back of his sleeve and said in a deep voice they had never heard before. *"Take it or leave it, boys!"*

Henry stuck out his hand and Mr. Parker slapped two dollars into his palm. "You bring some mink in here, then we'll talk money, boys!" His eyes fastened tightly to Henry's eyes and began to flare brighter red. He chomped harder on his tobacco.

"Come on, Robert!" Henry said. He grabbed Robert by the sleeve of his coat and quickly bolted to the door, never looking back. Outside, he leaned against the door and sighed a long sigh of relief.

Splat! He heard tobacco hit the inside of the door.

～

That evening Henry and Robert began their nightly trek to check their traps along Yankee Creek. Snow had fallen all day and by late evening six more inches covered the ground. There was no wind, just heavy snow. The usual night sounds of the woods had vanished with the thick snows. There were no usual screeches from night owls. No field mice scampered across the snows. And no deer stopped to lap the waters of Yankee Creek. In the stillness, they could almost hear the snowflakes slapping their chapped faces.

Though the sky was dark with heavy snow clouds, the new fallen snow emitted a dull halo of light as the beam from Henry's flashlight bobbed in front of their path.

Henry and Robert approached the first trap and Henry dropped to his knees in front of a muskrat hole. With his gloved hands, he brushed away the snow from around the trap. The beam from his flashlight told him there was nothing in the trap. Suddenly, a hand reached down and grabbed Henry's arm. Startled, Henry swirled around to see Robert kneeling at his side. "Did ya hear that?" Robert whispered.

"Hear what?" Henry whispered in return.

"I don't know!" Robert said more suspiciously. "It sounded like someone breathin' real hard out there toward Lovers' Lane!"

"Breathin' real hard?" Henry blurted back. He jumped to his feet and brushed the snow from his trousers. "Say! What are ya tryin' t' do, scare me like I scare you when I tell my stories at bedtime?" He paused and scanned the night air around him. "Well, it ain't gonna work, buster! Ya can't scare me!"

Nevertheless, Henry held his breath and perked his ears, his heart pounded wildly against his chest. "I don't hear nothin'!" he said. "You're just a sissy an'…" Suddenly, before Henry could finish his sentence, a blood-curdling scream echoed loudly from a nearby thicket. Then another horrible scream followed by another and still another came closer and louder.

"It's a woman!" Robert cried as he jumped to his feet. *"She's bein' murdered!"* And again a horrible scream sent shivers to Henry's and Robert's bones.

"Let's git outa here!" Henry shouted as he flung his remaining traps and flashlight wildly into the air and jumped a nearby blackberry bush.

Through the woods Henry and Robert darted under low branches and over wild thickets, hurrying to a dim light that shone from the faraway house.

In the freezing air, boiling sweat began to trickle down their faces. Slashing branches and blackberry bushes clawed angrily at their faces and clothing. Over a barbed-wire fence and past the outhouse they ran. Up the steps to the side porch and finally they burst through the kitchen door, slamming it quickly behind them. The harsh, bitter air and heavy running had stolen their breath and momentarily the two leaned safely against the kitchen door, unable to speak. As though it were the common thing to do, Robert snatched a chair from near the kitchen table and quickly propped it securely under the doorknob.

"What in the world is wrong with you two?" Mom blurted out as we all ran to the kitchen in surprise. "And why in the world did you prop that chair against the door?"

Robert took a deep breath and slid down the side of the door until he plopped to the floor below. His blue eyes were larger now. *"A woman was jist - jist - murdered in our woods t'night!"* He finally cried out, *"We heard her screamin' bloody murder somewhere in the direction of Lovers' Lane while we were checkin' our traps!"* He gasped for air and wiped his forehead with his stocking cap.

"He's right!" Henry added. *"Surely, she was bein' murdered right while we was there! I never heard nothin' like it in all my life!"* He fell to the floor and plopped beside Robert.

"Murdered?" I shouted. "In our woods?"

As though he were delirious, Henry stared frightfully into space. Then, still panting heavily, he spoke again. *"No doubt 'bout it! There wasn't nothin' we could do—so we jist ran for our lives!"*

Esther and Roberta stared wide-eyed with pale faces. Glen, too, looked frightened.

"Now, what in the world were you doing up by Lovers' Lane? You know I've told you at least a dozen times not to go near there!"

"We weren't near Lovers' Lane, Mom! We said the screamin' was comin' from there."

Wesley began to cry.

Mom wrapped her arms around Wesley and pulled him close. "Well, I doubt that someone was murdered in our woods. You probably got it in your minds that something bad is going to happen in Lovers' Lane because of what Aunt Rose and I keep telling you. However, if you say you heard screaming, I'll believe you."

"She was murdered, Mom! I tell ya she was murdered—right here in our woods!" Robert threw his coat to the floor.

Wesley stopped crying and Mom spoke again. "Well, I'm sure there's some explanation. Nevertheless, you kids get ready for bed and I'll tell your dad about it when he gets home from work. Go on, now, up those stairs!"

When Dad returned home from work we were all awake listening, once again to Henry's and Robert's tale of the woman being murdered in our woods. Downstairs, Mom began to tell Dad about the incident and then we heard Dad bust out with a loud roar of laughter. *"Woman?"* He laughed deep from the belly and slapped his knee. *"Murdered?"* He laughed louder. Finally, when the laughter stopped Dad's voice boomed. *"I'll bet my bottom dollar that wasn't no woman those boys heard! No sensible person is gonna be in Lovers' Lane this late at night, freezin' like it is. That was a bobcat! I guess I never told them about bobcats. Bobcats won't harm a flea unless they're cornered. But I have t' admit they do sound jist like a woman in distress when they cry out."* Once again he laughed loud and long. *"Woman! Murdered! Oh, boy! That's a good one!"*

Throughout the night we could hear Dad belly laugh again and again. Then we heard, *"Woman! Murdered! Ha! Ha! Ha!"*

The next day Aunt Rose and Uncle Clyde came to visit. They listened intently, as Henry and Robert retold their story of the woman who was murdered in our woods. They never said a word.

After supper, when Henry and Robert were coming from the barn, Aunt Rose was hanging bed sheets on the clothesline. Suddenly, there was a horrible scream behind the sheets. Henry and Robert stopped and stared suspiciously. Aunt Rose stuck her nose above the sheets and began to laugh loudly. "Seen any more murders lately, boys?" Then she laughed louder.

10 | Betty Jane

The first time we saw Betty Jane, she rode up our driveway sitting like an Indian, bareback on the most beautiful palomino horse in the whole wide world. Her long, blonde hair flowed down her back just like the coal black hair of a long-ago Indian. Her blue eyes sparkled like a sunset over the rippling waters of the Pacific Ocean.

"I'm Betty Jane," she said. "This is Jesse. She's my best friend." She smiled for the first time as she softly stroked the palomino's long neck. Her white teeth sparkled like a newly painted fence. "I live on a small knoll just up Anglin' Road a small piece." She pointed in the direction we had first seen smoke curling through the tall pines when as a family we had gathered at the window of Esther's and Roberta's bedroom and gazed across acres and acres of trees.

"You must live near Billy Johnson, my friend," Eddie said excitedly.

"Yes, I do. In fact, Billy's my neighbor." She looked to Eddie and smiled.

"I'm Esther, and these are my brothers and sisters," Esther said pointing to each of us. "We moved here only a short while ago. I don't remember seeing you in school."

"Well, I haven't been around here much myself. I've been living with my dad for a long, long time. But I sure am glad to be back here with Jesse again." She scratched the back of Jesse's neck. "I'll be riding the school bus now. I'm in the eighth grade."

"You're welcome to stay for awhile," Esther spoke. "We'll be having supper soon and we'd like to introduce you to Mom and our brother, Glen."

Once again, Betty Jane gently stroked Jesse's neck then rubbed between her ears. "That's very kind of you, but I'd best be getting home. Mom doesn't like me out too late, especially when it's getting dark. She's afraid of Bert Becker." Noticing the blank expressions on our faces, she spoke again. "You know Bert Becker, don't you?"

"Never heard of him," Roberta said. "Why? Who is he?"

"Me and Robert heard of him," Henry interrupted. "In fact, we seen him in the woods a few times. He has long white hair and a long white beard."

"His clothes look real old and tattered like he never changes them," Robert added.

"That's him all right," Betty Jane said.

The palomino reared her head, lifted her front legs into the air and snorted. "Whoa, girl!" Betty Jane said calmly. Again she stroked Jesse's neck, patting it softly. Jesse whinnied and then stood peacefully at Betty Jane's loving touch.

"Rumor has it that Bert Becker's wife up and left him one day, a long time ago, and ran off with another man. Bert Becker was so hurt that he went back into the woods, across the road from you, and built himself a little shack and stays there all by himself. He rarely comes out of the woods and never speaks to anyone. When I lived here before I used to see him on occasions, walking beside the road. But each time I got near him he ran into the woods. They say he usually comes out at night when nobody can see him. Mom says I'm never to go near him. She says she just doesn't trust anyone who acts the way he does."

"Wow! I feel sorry for him," Robert said. "I mean his wife left him for 'nother man. That has t' hurt."

Again the palomino shook her head and whinnied. "I guess Jesse's ready to go home," Betty Jane said. "It's getting late anyhow and I promised Mom I'd be home soon." She pulled the long mane that draped over Jesse's neck and the horse began to turn around. "I didn't mean to scare you about Bert Becker. I think he's a good man. Like Robert said, I think he's just a man who's deeply hurt and he's given up on life."

In a moment Jesse strutted down our driveway and then slowly galloped up Anglin' Road. Quickly, she and Betty Jane disappeared into the tall trees that lined Anglin' Road.

Mom was frying eggs when Dad appeared at the kitchen door the next morning. "Throw lots of bacon in that pan," Dad said with a grin. "I've got a busy day t'day and I don't know when I'll be able t' stop for lunch." He walked to the stove and gave Mom a big hug.

"The kids were talking all last evening about some old derelict living out in the woods across the road from us. Have you heard anything about him, Randall?"

"As a matter of fact, I have. Folks up in Hartford Center say he's harmless as a baby. Bert Becker, I think they call him. Why do you ask? What have the kids been sayin'?"

Mom slid the eggs and bacon onto Dad's plate. "They've been saying a lot of things. Things that I don't like, that's what I've been hearing."

"From what I hear, there's nothin' t' worry 'bout, Lydia. He's been around here for years and never harmed no one yet." Dad picked the sizzling bacon up with his fingers and took a bite. "You know how kids are. They let their imaginations run wild sometimes."

"Well, all I know is I don't want the girls running into him when they're on Anglin' Road or in our fields. Or the boys when they're out trapping, for that matter."

Dad began eating his breakfast and then spoke of the possibility of a cold rain in the air. He said he could feel it in his bones.

We talked little of either Bert Becker or Betty Jane in the days that followed. Often, I looked across Anglin' Road and gazed into the vast woods wondering where Bert Becker must live. Was his house made of tin? What did he eat? Did he have children and where did they live? I began seeing Betty Jane in school now and often she smiled and rubbed my head as she passed by. Once, Henry mentioned seeing Betty Jane in school and how pretty she looked. He said he wanted a horse some day and Robert teased him of wanting to go horseback riding with Betty Jane.

Then one day Betty Jane stopped in again. She dismounted her palomino and tied her to our side porch. "Just thought I would stop in and say hi," she said to Esther and Roberta as they stood on the side porch.

"You must be Betty Jane." Mom smiled through the screen door. "You're just as pretty as the children all said you were."

Betty Jane blushed. "Thank you, Ma'am."

"It's cold outside. Why don't you three come in and get warm. Glen will want to meet you anyhow, young lady." Then Mom held the door open while the three girls took their boots off and entered the house.

Betty Jane warmed her hands at the kitchen stove while Esther and Roberta took their coats off and hung them near the cellar entrance.

"Do you remember Bert Becker, the man I told you about when I last saw you?" she asked Esther and Roberta.

"Sure," both girls answered. "Why do you ask?"

"Well, I saw him yesterday just beyond the bridge and I thought of you two because he was so close to your house. Mind you now, they say he's harmless and he never has bothered me."

"Thank you for telling us that, Betty Jane," Mom interjected. "It's good that we know that. The girls need to keep their eyes open for anything and anybody unusual." She went to the stove and began stirring some hot chocolate. She poured the hot chocolate into three cups and gave each of the girls a cup. "You just be careful, too, young lady," Mom said to Betty Jane. "Just stay your distance."

"Oh, I will, Mrs. Stevenson. But I still believe he's harmless."

"Nevertheless," Mom uttered as she left the room and quickly returned pushing Glen's wheelchair across the kitchen threshold.

Betty Jane smiled to Glen and Glen smiled in return. "I heard you folks talking about this man, Bert Becker," Glen said, "and I just have a feeling he's just a lonely old man who's hurting so badly that he still blames himself for what happened to his marriage. I'll bet he feels unworthy of any kind of relationship with anyone."

Betty Jane smiled and said, "Our minds run the same course, Glen. I think you're absolutely right." Then she looked at the clock in the kitchen and said, "Oh, my goodness, I must be going now. I don't mean to rush off, but I did promise my mother I would help her with the supper tonight."

She slipped her gloves onto her hands and politely said good-bye as she smiled to Esther and Roberta. "It was a pleasure meeting you, Mrs. Stevenson. And you, too, Glen."

She opened the kitchen door, mounted Jesse, and the palomino trotted down the driveway and up Anglin' Road.

11 | The Best Farm Around

Occasionally, the cold days and long nights drew the failing strength from Glen's frail body and Doctor Higgins was called from nearby Sharpsville. From his black satchel the doctor withdrew his stethoscope, checked Glen's breathing, thumped on his chest with his knuckles, and shook his head in wonder.

"Keep him bundled up and keep him out of drafts," Doctor Higgins warned Mom as he left the house. "He must keep warm. That's where his strength lies now."

"The doctor says ya gotta keep warm, Glen. He says that's where your strength is," I said to Glen after the doctor left one day.

"I know," Glen replied. He was sitting up in his bed when he smiled to me. "But the doctor doesn't know where my real strength lies, does he?"

I wasn't sure what Glen meant by that remark. All I remember is that I went up to my bedroom and dug that lucky stone out of my sock drawer and whispered those same words to God about Glen singing in that musical.

Shortly after that, Glen began getting better. I wasn't sure why, but I was happy. And I started counting the days until he would sing in that musical.

Then one day the snows began to melt. The winds began to whisper instead of howl, and trees began to sing with blue birds, robins, and cardinals. Yellow dandelions poked their heads above the earth. And suddenly yellow, blue, pink, and purple wild flowers dotted the open fields. Brown squirrels stuck their lazy heads out of their tree nests, sniffed the warm air, and began chattering loudly. Spring had finally arrived.

"We'll plant field corn in those five acres over there," Dad said as he pointed to the grassy field lying in the west corner of the farm. "I decided t' try plantin' an acre of potatoes in the open field behind the barn. It's pretty sandy soil an' I think it should produce a good crop."

Then, as Mom pushed Glen in his wheelchair down the long driveway, we all followed and listened as Dad began to tell of his plans to renovate the low, flat shanty beside the driveway and convert it into a chicken coop. "It's the best place t' begin a new farm," he said. "Plenty of eggs an' lots of fine feathered friends will make a healthy family," he added.

Next, he told of his plans of owning cows and pigs someday and of building the farm into one of the best around. "But it'll take time, Lydia. It won't be done over night. But we'll do it. I promise you."

His eyes were sharp and convincing and Mom believed him as she always did. Dad was a hard worker. Everybody knew that. Uncle Clyde had often said that Dad was going to work his way into an early grave working as hard as he did. But that was Dad's way of life. He acquired the habit of rising early each morning and working until sundown as a young boy in the Boys' Home. It was a pattern he would follow religiously for the remainder of his life.

Early one morning, Billy Johnson came to visit. He was sitting at the kitchen table with our family when Dad announced that it was time to get serious about farming. "Now, Billy, you can stay if you want t' or you can go home. But we've got a lot of work t' do around here. I don't want t' be rude so you make the choice." Dad got up from the table and walked to the kitchen door.

"Oh, no, Mr. Stevenson, you're not being rude. I'd like to help if I may."

Dad looked to Mom and then smiled. "Did you ever see a group of kids like these on Anglin' Road, Lydia?" Then he put his hat on and went out the kitchen door.

With Eddie, Billy, and me assigned to cleaning out the low, flat shanty that sat next to the driveway, Dad, Henry, and Robert began digging holes around the shanty and placing long, slender poles into each hole. Next, they strung chicken wire from one pole to another, attached the ends to two sides of the shanty, and nailed the wire firmly to the poles with "u" shaped nails.

Then, Dad took Eddie, Billy, and me to the edge of the woods where a grove of small, quaking aspen trees crowded together. "Step back an' keep clear of the flying chips," he said as he pulled his sharp hatchet from his belt and began chopping the long slender trees. Each tree was only about an inch and one half in diameter and cut to a length not to exceed eight feet. Next, Dad trimmed each tree of its few branches until it became a long, straight pole. When Dad finished trimming the poles he placed his hatchet into his belt and began piling the poles into our outstretched arms.

Eddie, Billy, and I carried these poles back to the new chicken coop where Dad proceeded to arrange them together so they resembled a short, wide ladder. Then, tying them together with binder twine, he set one end of the wide ladder in the middle of the floor, propped the other end against the far wall, and nailed it firmly in place.

"These," Dad said, "are the chicken roosts. Chickens are like other birds an' like t' perch upon limbs. As soon as it gets dark, they'll all come into the chicken coop an' perch upon these roosts. Now, follow me t' the barn an' we'll please the chickens with some fancy nests t' lay their eggs."

In the barn, Dad handed Eddie and me two orange crates apiece and then he picked up four more and headed back to the chicken coop. "These are their nests," he said as he nailed them to the walls about four feet from the floor. "We'll fill each one with straw and when they're ready t' lay their eggs they'll just fly up here an' cuddle in the straw an' lay their solid gold eggs!" He laughed and pretended he would hit Eddie in the nose with his hammer. Quickly, Eddie jumped back and laughed in return. "Well, if they lay enough eggs it will be like gold anyways," he concluded. "Now, you three get busy and fill these nests an' then spread some straw around the floor. For some reason, chickens prefer havin' carpet on their floors."

At the supper table Mom set a plate for Billy and slid another chair between Eddie and me. "You'll eat here today after working so hard in that chicken coop all day," she said.

"Oh, no, Mrs. Stevenson! I can't do that! My mother said you have enough kids to feed without one more. She told me to politely excuse myself and come on home."

Mom laughed loudly. "Well, I think she'll excuse you this one time," she said and scooped some mashed potatoes onto his plate.

After supper, Dad loaded some old chicken crates on top of the Willys and he, Henry, and Robert drove off to a large chicken farm, somewhere in Pennsylvania. In the late evening they returned and in the chicken crates were ten of the noisiest, most cackling chickens in the whole wide world and one cocky rooster.

Once again we all gathered around the Willys as Dad began to unload the chickens and set them behind the new fence.

"Just look at that rooster," Esther said. "He sure thinks he's king around here already!"

"Why not call him King Tut?" Glen said. "I think King Tut had a large harem like this rooster does, didn't he?"

"I'm sure he did," Dad laughed. "King Tut it is." Then looking to Mom, he said, "This farm is beginnin' t' take shape, Lydia. Soon we'll have a cow. You can bet your bottom dollar on that! An' before long those fields will be bustin' loose with the finest crops you ever laid your eyes on." He paused and leaned against the fence to watch the chickens flapping and cackling in their new pen. Proudly, he took a deep breath of the wonderful country air surrounding him. "But the next thing we're gonna do is get ourselves another car, Lydia." He chuckled as he obviously surprised Mom and us children with his sudden decision.

"Now, Randall! We don't need a new car right now," Mom pleaded. "The old Willys will do just fine. The children and I want you to get that tractor first, Randall. Without it we won't have a farm."

But there was no use in Mom's plea. We could all tell by the twinkle in Dad's eyes that he would not change his mind. We had all seen that look so many times before and we knew there was more on his mind than he was revealing and Mom told him so. "You might as well come clean right now, Randall. You've got something up your sleeve and you might as well tell us now."

All around we waited excitedly as Dad began to speak. First he chuckled and leaned against the new fence, now laughing as two chickens squabbled over silly nothings. Then, pulling Mom toward him he pointed toward the old Willys. "That, my dear young lady, is our new tractor!" And again he chuckled as though she should have known.

But Mom looked surprised. "Randall," she said with a puzzled look on her face, "I just can't understand an old car suddenly becoming a tractor." Still, if ever her faith were in anybody to perform such a feat, it would be Dad. So many times she had seen him do the unbelievable.

"We're gonna get a car, Lydia, because I can kill two birds with one stone. You see, the car's a seven-passenger Plymouth. It seats two in the front, three in the back, an' there are two seats in the middle that fold up an' down. It's just what we need for our family. It's in real good shape, too. An', I don't think I have t' tell you that I've made a good deal on it. In fact, I made such a good deal that I honestly feel a little guilty about it right now," Dad said. But he winked at Glen to let us know he was only kidding about feeling guilty. And we all knew it was a good deal too, for we remembered how Mr. Clayton, our neighbor in Brookfield, had stormed off and said he would not take a penny less than one hundred and twenty-five dollars for the old Willys just before we moved to Hartford. But the next day Dad paid him one hundred dollars and talked him into throwing in two more tires and a set of tire chains to boot. And Uncle Clyde often teased that Dad could talk a baby into giving him his or her candy.

"I'm gonna strip the Willys down an' convert it into a tractor, Lydia. Believe me, it's still got plenty of pep. It'll make a perfect tractor."

"Well, I do declare, Randall! You never cease to amaze me. But somehow I believe you." Mom wiped her hands on her apron and smiled at Glen as though in disbelief.

By the middle of the following week the new car had arrived. Dad had risen early in the morning and picked up Uncle Clyde in Brookfield. While Uncle Clyde drove the old Willys back home Dad had the honor of showing off the new seven-passenger Plymouth. What a proud moment as Dad pulled up the long driveway, blowing the horn, inviting us all to come see the new car. "Of course it's not a brand new car," Dad boasted. "In fact, it's nearly ten years old. But 'longside the old Willys it looks brand new. An' just look how streamlined it looks compared to the old Willys."

Immediately, the seven of us ascended upon the Plymouth examining the dashboard, the horn, the space, the soft seats, and the two seats in the middle that folded up and down. Dad pounded on the front fender. "Solid as a brick outhouse!" he declared. "An' jist look at those tires! Ten thousand miles left on that tread or I'll eat my hat."

"Mighty fine deal!" Uncle Clyde declared as he and Dad lifted both sides of the hood. "Sure is a mighty fine deal!"

"Start her up, Robert," Dad said as his head rose above the raised hood. "I want Clyde t' hear how smooth this engine purrs."

Both men leaned against opposite fenders. Robert sat behind the steering wheel, smiled to Henry who was seated next to him, turned the key, and pushed the start button. The engine gave one crank, jumped forward, and threw both men up into the air.

"*What in blue blazes are you doin'?*" Dad yelled when the car stopped. "Push the stupid clutch in first, *then* put the car in neutral. *I thought you knew better than that!*"

Uncle Clyde backed away and then started laughing. "If I didn't know better, I'd swear that was Aunt Rose behind the wheel," he said. Once again he lifted his pants with his wrists and laughed louder.

Robert started the car smoothly, put the emergency brake on and gripped the steering wheel with both hands. Dad and Uncle Clyde leaned across the fenders and Henry reached across and tooted the horn. Ooga! Ooga! The horn blared loudly.

Dad and Uncle Clyde jumped suddenly and hit their heads against the hood of the car. Red-faced and angered, Dad pulled himself from under the hood and glared viciously at Robert. He picked his hat off the engine and placed it back upon his head. "*Now what in tarnation's name are you doin'? Get out of that car right now!*" he yelled to Robert. Then he slammed the hood down and shooed us all away from the car.

The next day Uncle Clyde arrived early. Dad drove the Willys into the barn and the two men began to strip the Willys. First, the fenders were torn off to make it look more like a tractor. Besides, Uncle Clyde said the fenders would only get in the way and gather mud. Next, the roof was chopped off, and then different wheels were put on. Then the doors were taken off. Day by day different modifications were added to the engine and the body.

Then one day Dad walked around the new tractor and studied it very closely. Once again, he kicked the tires. He cranked the engine and listened to its soft rumble. He revved the engine. Finally, he stepped back and smiled to Uncle Clyde. "You know, Clyde, I believe we have somethin' here. I believe that looks like a tractor. Don't you?"

"There's one-way to find out, Randall," Uncle Clyde said. "Let's hook it up to that dusty plow of yours and see what it can do."

"Do ya think it will work?" Eddie asked. He shielded his eyes from the setting sun.

"Of course it'll work," Henry said. "If Dad says it'll work, it'll work!"

Dad jumped up to the lone seat in the new tractor and backed up to the plow. "Hook her up, Clyde."

Uncle Clyde guided the tongue of the plow to the back of the tractor and slipped a long bolt through the hole to lock it in place. Slapping the back of the tractor as though it were the rear of a horse, he chuckled and said, "Go get 'em, girl!"

In a moment the new tractor was chugging down the field dragging the long plow behind, while all around, we children danced for joy. As he passed Uncle Clyde on his way back up the field, Dad waved from the odd looking tractor. "There's more than one way t' skin a cat!" He hollered. And the plow dug deep, turning the fresh, sweet-smelling earth into long, even furrows.

Mom smiled and looked to Aunt Rose. "He never ceases to amaze me," she said.

Glen tugged at the knee of his pants and gradually elevated his scrawny leg until the heel of his shoe dug into the front of the wheelchair seat. With his foot now resting comfortably on the edge of the seat, Glen winked at Mom and returned a glance at the distant tractor. "Somehow, I think we're going to have the best farm around," he said.

12 | Teddy—A Gift From God

When Dad released the news at the supper table, that there would soon be two new members to the farm, we were so excited we could barely eat. How long we had waited to own a cow! Now there would be two of them!

"They're both Holsteins," Dad said excitedly while he reached across the table for another slice of bread. "But one's a bull. I expect t' get ten quarts a milkin' from the cow, though," he boasted. He spread butter across his bread while we listened attentively. "Mr. Clark claims Holsteins give more milk than most other cows. No doubt, with a family this size, that's exactly what we need. Of course we're gonna need someone t' take care of them." His eyes stole a glance to Henry and Robert and with a wink of his eye Dad exclaimed, "She'll have t' be milked twice a day, boys. Of course I'll be able t' milk her each mornin', but she'll need milkin' every evenin' at the same time. Cows can't wait t' be milked. She'll expect you every evenin' at the same time."

"We know, Dad," Henry spoke up. "We'll be there every evenin'. You can count on us."

Dad rose from the table. Taking the last swallow of his piece of bread, he walked to the bucket of water at the sink and lifted a dipper full of water. "I know I can, Henry," he returned while he put the dipper of water to his lips. "I've learned t' count on everybody 'round here."

"I have names picked out for them already, Dad," Glen declared. And before any of us could even begin to think what they might be Glen said, "Daisy Mae and Li'l Abner."

Mom began to clear the table and joined Dad at the sink. "My goodness!" She laughed. "First we have King Tut. Now it's Daisy Mae and Li'l Abner. Who will it be next?"

"Porky Pig!" Glen said quickly. "I've already thought of a pig."

"Well," Dad said as we all began to laugh, "you're always one step ahead of me."

Dad tossed the dipper back into the water bucket, walked past Glen, and ruffled his hair. Looking to Henry, he spoke again. "Since Mr. Clark lives only 'a frog's jump away', you, me, an' Robert will walk up Anglin' Road t' his farm and lead Daisy Mae and Li'l Abner back with ropes. The rest of you can wait at the wooden bridge." He slipped his hat on and stepped to the side porch. "It won't be safe t' have the cows confronted with so much excitement at first. There ain't any children on Mr. Clark's farm so Daisy Mae and Li'l Abner might get temperamental when they see all of you at one time," he warned us. The porch door slammed behind him as he stepped outside.

The next morning Dad, Henry, and Robert left for Mr. Clark's farm. With ropes in hand they wandered up Anglin' Road and out of view. Later, when we thought they should be returning, Esther and Roberta pushed Glen to the wooden bridge while Eddie, Wesley, and I followed. Excitement welled up inside each of us as we sat upon the railings of the bridge waiting for the first signs of Daisy Mae and Li'l Abner.

"They'll be here any minute now, I'll betcha," Glen declared. "And don't hang over the bridge so far or you'll fall in!" He shouted to Wesley as Wesley leaned across the guard rail; his eyes glued to a school of fish swimming under the bridge. But Glen's warning was too late. As the last fish flipped its tail and swam under the bridge, Wesley leaned just beyond the point of no return.

"Look out!" Glen screamed. But Wesley's scream was louder as he tumbled over the bridge and plunged helplessly toward the water below.

There was nothing to do now except listen for the splash and pray that one of us could reach Wesley before the waters below enveloped his body and snuffed his very breath from his living soul. But miraculously, Wesley's tiny fingers somehow grasped the bridge support and now he dangled helplessly while his feet kicked hopelessly through thin air.

"Help! Help!" he screamed. "I'm drownin'! I'm drownin'!"

Quickly, Esther and Roberta raced to Wesley. In near despair, they grasped him firmly by his wrists. "Thank goodness!" Roberta said. "That was too close!" Carefully she and Esther lifted him to the bridge above.

"I'm drownin'! I'm drownin'!" Wesley continued to cry as the girls set his swinging feet to the bridge below.

"Oh, settle down, now!" Esther chuckled in relief as Wesley refused to open his eyes. "You're not even near the water, so how in the world can you be drowning!"

Cautiously, Wesley opened his eyes. "Here comes Li'l Abner an' Daisy Mae!" He smiled now as he wiped his eyes with the back of his fists.

In the far distance, Li'l Abner and Daisy Mae crisscrossed Anglin' Road with Henry and Robert close behind. Now and then they stopped to munch the luscious, green grass alongside the road. Then, twitching their heads, they swished their tails and soon they were galloping full speed down Anglin' Road with Henry and Robert clinging to the long ropes behind.

"Hold them back, boys!" Dad commanded as he trailed behind with a long stick. "Don't let them run so!"

At the sound of Dad's commanding voice, Daisy Mae and Li'l Abner trotted aimlessly to the side of the road. Once again their hungry tongues began to lash at the tall, green grasses. Pulling the grass from its roots, they lifted their heads high above their gangly bodies. Back and forth their lower jaws munched the sweet, green grasses while their long tails swished happily back and forth. Satisfied, they once again waddled slowly to the bridge ahead.

Anxiously we waited at the wooden bridge, careful not to excite the approaching cows.

"Careful now!" Dad called. "The sound of their own hoofs on the bridge might frighten them. Be extra careful now, boys. We don't want them t' panic. You kids back off the bridge now! We don't want nothin' t' scare them."

Quickly, we heeded to Dad's instructions. With Esther on one side and Roberta on the other they guided Glen's wheelchair safely from the pressing cows.

Steadily, Henry and Robert pulled at the taut ropes.

"Whoa! Steady now!" Henry called as Li'l Abner jerked his head at the hollow sound of the bridge below. "Easy does it!"

Suddenly, a wild rustling sound came from the weeds near the bridge. In the twinkling of an eye a strange animal sprang from the weeds like a wild tiger and began nipping at the heels of Li'l Abner. In a flash, Li'l Abner reared his head, pulled his long rope from Henry's hands, and stampeded back up Anglin' Road with Daisy Mae following close behind.

"*It's a dog!*" Glen shouted as Henry and Robert chased after the runaway cows. "Come here, boy!" He called to the dog.

"Now where in the world did he come from?" Dad asked as the thin, red dog stood with watchful eyes.

"Come on, boy!" Glen continued to call.

"You'd better not call him, Glen," I said. "He might be mean."

"He's not mean. Anyone can see that. He's just starvin', that's all. Just look at his ribs stickin' out so! I'll bet he hasn't eaten in a week. The poor thing! Just look how pathetic he looks! And he could be so beautiful with that red coat." Glen puckered his lips and whistled to the red dog.

Now the dog's tail wagged excitedly as he begged for attention. Dad slowly edged toward the red dog. The dog's ears drooped low, his tail curled beneath his legs, and quickly he backed away and slipped into the weeds.

"Part German Shepherd, no doubt," Dad said as he took the rope from Henry and carefully guided Li'l Abner across the bridge. "Prob'ly dropped off by somebody who didn't want him no more."

"Who would do a thing like that?" Roberta asked and shook her head in disbelief.

"Lots of people do that kinda stuff," Robert hollered back as Daisy Mae set her hoofs hard to the wooden bridge and the deep hollow sounds thundered across the water. "They don't have no heart, that's why."

Daisy Mae thumped across the wooden bridge behind Li'l Abner. Her head high, her tail swishing back and forth, she snorted and shook her head.

Dad handed Li'l Abner's rope back to Henry and followed the two boys and Li'l Abner and Daisy Mae up the driveway and to the barn.

For a long time Dad, Robert, and Henry worked in the barn setting up the new stables and getting familiar with the new members of the farm. An occasional laughter mixed with the soft lowing of the cows came from the barn.

I stood at the front door of the barn and stared back at Glen who was now seated on the side porch. Was he thinking, like I was, about the stray, red dog? What would become of it? How would it live with no one to care for it? Then, as if my very thoughts had made it appear, the stray dog stood at the side porch and stared sadly up at Glen. With a soft whimper the red dog curled his tail and then wagged it pleadingly. Excitedly, I ran to the side porch to be with Glen.

Suddenly Glen's eyes were aglow. "Come here, boy! Come on now!" He begged as he puckered his lips and blew a soft whistle.

Slowly, the red dog climbed the steps to the side porch, inching closer and closer to Glen. Timid and afraid, the dog whimpered softly and cautiously nudged Glen's chair.

" 'At a boy! Come on!" Glen whispered.

With sad eyes the red dog lapped at Glen's hand. His tail wagged vigorously. "That's a good boy!" Glen whispered again.

The red dog raised itself on its hind legs and rested its front paws upon the arm of Glen's wheelchair. Glen tilted his head toward the dog and the dog lapped excitedly at Glen's face.

"My goodness!" Mom spoke through the screen door. "What have we here? Where did that dog come from?"

"He followed us home from the bridge, Mom," Glen said as he rubbed his hand gently across the dog's head. "He's starvin', Mom. Can we give him some milk?"

Mom smiled as the side door slammed behind her. "Such a timely question," she said. "Heaven knows we'll have plenty of milk now. I guess we can afford some."

Mom set the warm milk in front of the dog and his tongue lapped like wildfire, pausing only to thank Mom for her kindness.

"Can we keep him, Mom? He won't be any trouble. And what's one more animal around here?" Glen asked. His green eyes sparkled.

"Well, now! Just look at this, would you! It looks like we don't have any choice now, do we?" Mom beamed as the dog crawled under Glen's chair, circled three times, and curled into a soft ball. His sad eyes looked up to Mom and thanked her once again.

"I'm gonna call him Teddy, Mom. How's that sound? He reminds me of a skinny Teddy bear."

Teddy wagged his tail briskly and looked up with sheepish eyes. With the assurance that all was well, he twitched his head, rested his lower jaw upon his two front paws, and peacefully closed his eyes.

"I do declare!" Mom said. "I think he's found a home!"

From the barn, Daisy Mae and Li'l Abner lowed once again. Teddy lifted his eyes to the distant sound, and when it faded with the passing breeze, he gave a soft whimper and quietly closed his eyes.

Mom leaned against the pillar of the side porch and folded her arms together. "Those cows are just the ticket," she said to Esther and Roberta as they joined Mom and Glen on the side porch. "They mean the world to your dad." Turning to face the two girls directly, she continued. "Remember how your dad promised to build a good farm, the best around?" She reached down and held Glen's hand. Then she stared at the distant barn. "Well, if you ask me, God surely has blessed us. Just look at the joy a stray dog has planted in Glen's heart. Surely this dog has been God-sent! Did you know, for a fact, that's exactly what the name Teddy means - God sent?" Now she gazed upon the vast domain encircling the old, timeworn house. "Perhaps it's all a part of God's great master plan," she said.

13 | The Bear That Stalked Anglin' Road

That evening the kerosene lamp flickered, high on the dresser top, while the warm summer breeze slipped through the open bedroom windows and teased the golden flame. I tossed and turned in my bed. I would not fall to sleep easily for now my head whirled with excitement. I thought of Daisy Mae and Li'l Abner and goose bumps pricked my skin. I thought of Glen with Teddy and I felt good all over. I recalled how Mom had assured us that Teddy was surely 'God-sent' since the very name Glen had chosen for the dog meant exactly that. I had heard of miracles before, but never had I been so close to one! And surely this was a miracle since Glen was so full of life for the first time since we had left Brookfield. And I remembered, too, how Mom, at the first sight of our new house, had longed to return to Brookfield. But now that she could see Dad's dream coming true she wanted more than ever to stay here on Anglin' Road.

How happy I was now that we had moved to Hartford! It was not the kind of house most people would like to live in, since there was no running water or electricity and no inside toilet. But there was something here that electrified my soul even though I could not explain why.

"Will you tell us 'nother story t'night, Esther?" I called across the gray shadows of the bedroom. "I don't think I can sleep t'night."

"Yeah, tell us 'nother story 'bout Har'furd!" Wesley agreed. "Dose are da best kind!"

"Okay," Esther beamed as she sat up in her bed. She pulled her knees up to her chin, flicked her long curls behind her shoulders, and wrapped the light blanket close to her neck. Then she spoke again. "If everyone is in favor of it, I'll tell you a real good story about something that happened just up the road from us, right here on Anglin' Road."

"Okay!" We all chorused, as we snuggled cozily into positions suited for a long story.

I placed my elbows deep into the mattress and rested my head comfortably in the palms of my hands. Eddie and Wesley squirmed beneath the covers and burrowed to the far end of their bed until, soon, both heads popped above the covers and quietly they waited for Esther to begin. Robert closed his eyes and cupped his hands behind his head. Roberta pulled herself close to Esther as she always did during Esther's stories.

Presently, the large dimly-lit room was filled with a dead silence, so still we could almost hear the soft, golden flames of the kerosene lamp as they flickered and waved with the warm summer breeze blowing through the open windows. From the small cot in the middle of the boys' bedroom a faint snore rose from Henry's lips and then died with the passing breeze.

"A long, long, time ago, long before there were busses to pick up the boys and girls for school, they used to use horses and buggies in Hartford," Esther began. "In those days Hartford was a very small school - so small there were only about forty kids in the entire school. And one of those kids was a young boy named Seth Thomas."

"Was he related t' the Thomas family that lives in Hartford now?" I interrupted.

"Yes, he was. In fact he was the great grandfather of Mr. Charles Thomas."

"Wow! That's a long time ago!" Eddie chimed in.

"Well," Esther continued, "it seems that some men had somehow captured a giant bear one day and locked it up in a shed at the corner of Anglin' Road and Route 7. After school one day, Seth Thomas started to get on the wagon to ride home and then thought, 'If I go home on the wagon I won't get to see the bear, so I'll just walk home.' So he started to walk home."

"Didn't the driver make him ride the wagon home?" Eddie asked.

"Would ya guys quit interruptin' so she can git on with the story?" Robert snapped.

Henry began snoring much louder now.

"Can't we put a muzzle or somethin' over Henry's nose so we can hear the story?" Eddie asked, a bit perturbed at Henry's unnecessary snoring.

"Maybe if we put a pillow over him he'll git quiet," I suggested.

"That's not funny, Carl!" Roberta called from the girls' bedroom. "You could kill somebody that way!"

"For Pete's sake! Do you guys want to hear this story or not?" Esther pleaded.

Once again all became quiet, except for Henry's snoring, which had fortunately subsided somewhat by now.

"As he got to Anglin' Road, Seth decided to go to the shed and look at the bear and talk to it for awhile. He walked around the shed, peeking through the cracks and saying things to it. But suddenly it growled and tried to snatch his fingers, which he would stick through the cracks and then quickly pull back - *barely in time.*

"Then, after about ten minutes, Seth decided he'd better hurry home before his mom and dad became worried, so he started down Anglin' Road at a good pace, kicking stones and whistling. Every once in awhile he would stoop to pick a stone up and fling it at a nearby target and then scoot along a little faster. There were no houses between the corner and their house - which incidentally is the same house that Mr. Harold Thomas lives in now."

"Gosh!" I interrupted again. "That's a long way t' walk by yourself! And that's not far from here!"

"There were tree stumps in the road then because there were no cars and the wagons just rolled over and around the stumps. Every once in awhile Seth would stop to catch his breath and rest on one of those stumps. He didn't know it, *but,*"—Esther's voice began to crack—"the bear had broken out of the shed just after Seth was there and was now *following him!*"

"Oh, my gosh!" Eddie blurted out. "What did he do then?"

"Well, every time he would stop and rest, the bear would stop. Two men realized, immediately, that the bear had escaped and set out quickly to find it. Fortunately, they came upon it real fast! But now the bear was so close to Seth that they were afraid to do anything. If they tried to shoot it, they might miss and the bear might attack Seth!

"Once again, Seth began walking and the bear followed—each time taking bigger steps than Seth that drew him closer and closer. Every time that Seth would stop, the bear would stop. And every time the bear stopped, the men stopped. On and on this pursuit went. And soon it began getting dark because the sun was slowly sinking. Now the men were hoping that Seth would hurry home before it became too dark to see the bear."

"Why din't dey yell at da boy an' tell him t' run?" Wesley asked, clinging to the foot of the bed.

"They couldn't yell at him because that would only frighten the boy and alarm the bear. All they could do now was follow and hope the boy would get home before dark," Esther answered.

"For nearly half an hour more this pursuit continued. Then, shortly before dark, Seth finally walked into his front yard and entered his house—*unaware that close behind followed a giant bear.*

"The two men watched the bear very closely as it stalked the front door, as though it might charge the house and burst through the door. Then, just before the sun set below the horizon, the two men fired their guns and killed the bear in Seth's front yard."

"Wow!" Eddie said, swallowing a lump in his throat. "That was a close call!"

"When Seth and his dad ran outside, at the sound of the shots, they were amazed to see the bear. And what's more - they were terrified to hear the story the men had to tell!

"And that happened just up the road - less than half a mile from here," Esther concluded.

"Boy! Dat was a good story, Esther," Wesley said, crawling under his cover. "Dere sure was a lotta nice thin's dat happened here in Har'furd, wasn't dere?"

"There sure were, Wesley," Esther agreed, yawning. "But now it's time to go to sleep."

Slipping the cover over the foot of the bed, Esther whisked across the floor and blew across the glass chimney of the kerosene lamp, snuffing the once golden flames. "Goodnight, boys," she whispered as she set the lamp carefully upon the dresser top.

"Goodnight," I returned with a sleepy yawn. "Thanks for tellin' that story, Esther. It sure was an excitin' one! Imagine that! A giant bear like that actually walkin' down this road! An' not far from our house!"

"Hmm, hmm," Esther yawned again.

I closed my eyes, and soon the deep silence surrounded me as the thought of a giant bear prowling Anglin' Road seemed ever so haunting. Outside the bedroom window, nestled in a lost thicket, a lonely cricket called to a nearby bullfrog. In the far distance a train rumbled across the trestle of the railroad tracks and its mournful whistle seemed to call, *"Come with me! Come with me!"* And my eyes became helplessly heavy.

With the last whistle fading into the distant hills, the lonely cricket tenderly chirped itself to a pleasant sleep. The fat bullfrog swallowed the large bag of air in his throat and called it a night. Now, all that existed was the soft, summer breeze flowing through the open windows and the dull hum of a sleepy house.

14 | The Strange Intruder

"What was that?" Eddie rose up in bed and sat wide-eyed gazing fearfully through the pitch of the night. His pale face stiffened at the frightening sounds coming from the dark room next to our bedroom.

"I don't know!" Robert whispered. "Somethin's in the other room!"

"What's going on out there?" Esther called from the girls' bedroom.

Robert gulped, and then took a long breath. "We don't know," he said. "Somethin's in the room next t' ours!"

"Maybe it's one of those ghosts that Henry's always tellin' us 'bout," I uttered.

Swish! Bang! Thud! The noises grew louder.

"I saw a ghost in dere da udder night!" Wesley said, and then shook in his bed like Teddy shaking water off his back.

"You saw no such thing, Wesley!" Roberta bellowed from the girls' bedroom. "There are no such things as ghosts!"

Still, Roberta snuggled closer to Esther and wrapped the thin blankets firmly around her body. And now we waited anxiously while the strange intruder planned its next frightening move.

Presently, there was a long silence, like the silence of a graveyard at midnight, while Esther slipped from the covers and hurriedly lit the kerosene lamp. Carefully, she set the lamp upon the dresser top and then, with lightning speed, she scurried to the comforts of the brass bed where she snuggled close to Roberta. "You're right, Roberta, there's no such things as ghosts," I heard her whisper to Roberta as she crawled into bed.

Crash! Bang! Swish! The sounds came louder and nearer now. Suddenly, with a loud thud, the door to the dark room burst wide open. Past the door a strange body tumbled across the floor and rolled aimlessly in the direction of the stairs. In its hand a large broom waved fiercely while the grotesque body seemed to be chasing madly after something high above.

"*It's Henry!*" Robert shouted in relief.

"*Cover your heads!*" Mom yelled as she entered the bedroom behind Henry, frantically waving a small flashlight. "*There's a bat in your bedroom!*"

"E-e-e-e-e !" Esther and Roberta squealed with a bloodcurdling scream that reverberated through the rooms, bouncing off the bare walls. Chills ran up and down my spine and once again my breath was hard to find.

High above Henry and flying more aimlessly fluttered the largest and ugliest bat known to mankind. Down toward Robert's head it dipped and then fluttering around the room it veered just in time from hitting the walls and ceiling, nearly bumping the lamp that rested on the tall dresser.

Quickly, Henry sprang from the floor of the bedroom and commenced to swirl the long broom high above his head, swishing at the strange intruder. Large gusts of swirling winds rippled from Henry's broom chasing wild flames that cast giant shadows across the wall, resembling the ferocious pterodactyls of prehistoric times. Small shadows grew quickly into larger shadows and then back to smaller shadows as the bat fluttered back and forth in front of the glowing lamp. Closer and closer the shadows swooped over us, draining every ounce of strength from our terrified bodies. Down toward Wesley's head the bat swooped again. But just in time, Wesley's reflexes responded as quickly he darted under the covers.

"Keep your heads down, I said! It could be rabid!" Mom shouted with a commanding voice.

Back and forth Henry ran, swishing the broom. Up and down the bat fluttered. Larger and larger the shadows on the walls grew, becoming more and more grotesque as they paraded up and down and back and forth. Again Henry swung his broom. But once again he missed the speedy bat. Thud! The broom banged against the dresser, and this time the broom nearly hit the hideous intruder.

"Be careful of the lamp!" Mom shouted at the top of her voice, rushing to seize the kerosene lamp from its rocky motion.

Swish! Swish! Swish! The broom hissed as it swirled through the somber room.

Thud! Bang! Crunch! The walls echoed again as Henry swung in desperation, reaching over the sturdy banister at the top of the steps.

"I got 'em!" Henry finally bellowed as his nimble body tumbled across the banister and the long broom nipped the bat with its last swish of the air.

"Be careful!" Mom cried again. In an instant she lunged forward, stretching her petite body beyond all reasonable distance, grasping Henry by his waist while his lanky body plunged to the depths below.

"I think I got 'em, Mom!" Henry called breathlessly. *"I think he's on the bottom step!"*

Pulling Henry's dangling body safely across the banister; Mom shone the light at the steps below until the narrow beam focused on the wounded bat below. *"Thank goodness!"* She sighed in relief. *"It's finally over!"*

From the fortress of our beds we sprang wildly, racing toward the banister to set our eyes upon the fallen intruder.

But Esther and Roberta were much more cautious as they wrapped their shivering bodies with the warm, brown blanket and cautiously slipped from their bed, peeking nervously around the doorway of their tiny bedroom. From a safe distance, four eyes, the size of small saucers, protruded wearily through the brown lump of covers.

"Is it dead?" the brown lump asked fearfully.

Bang! The broom struck again with lightning quickness. "It is now, I betchya!" Henry assured the brown lump as he put the finishing touches on the still body. *"Hey! He's really ugly! Ya guys wanna see him close up?"* he asked, scooping the ghastly figure with the bristles of his broom.

"E-e-e-e-e-!" The girls squealed as Henry lifted the bat suddenly upward, toward the screaming brown lump, and with the speed of two fleeting cheetahs the girls fled to the refuge of their tiny bedroom.

"Nothing doing, Henry! Just carry that thing outside this instant and throw it into the high weeds! *And I mean right now!*" Mom ordered, pointing to the door at the foot of the steps.

Robert stretched his neck across the banister and took a last look at the bat as Henry carried it past the door. "How do ya s'pose a bat got in here?" he asked.

"It probably came down from the attic," Mom replied. "It could be full of bats after all these years. But now it's nearly time for your dad to return from work, so off to bed with all of you. And don't say a word about this to your dad. The Good Lord knows he's got plenty to think about without worrying about bats. I'll tell him when the right time comes." She took a long shiver, a good sigh of relief, and motioned for us to hurry back to bed.

"It's a kinda spooky house if ya ask me," Wesley said as he scanned the gray shadows flickering across the bedroom walls and then pulled the covers directly over his head. "Me and bats never did git' long." The muffled sounds came from under the covers.

"I'll bet we have the only house around with bats in it," I boasted.

"That's really an honor, Carl. It's something to really be proud of!" Roberta teased sarcastically, and then leaned back in her bed.

"I'll betcha years later we'll look back at this an' think how nice it was, though," I replied. But once again there was no reply as sleepy children shunned the ghastly thought with a care less yawn.

Quietly, Esther snuffed the golden flames from the kerosene lamp and once again I was left alone to ponder the exciting events that would someday be fond memories of the old house on Anglin' Road.

15 | The Stranger

Across the front yard, and up and down trees, brown squirrels busily dashed in and out, picking up acorns, packing their food ever so carefully and gingerly in the far corners of their tree houses. On the ground, smaller chipmunks scurried here and there, much in the same fashion, tucking their treasures away in some dark corner of a secret hole near the well in the back yard. Then, time and time again, they returned to repeat this same ritual. For hours on end they scampered here and there, busily preparing for the long, hard winter that lay ahead. Dad, Henry, and Robert stood beside the barn watching the squirrels.

"Animals seem t' know when a hard winter's comin', boys, an' they never rest till all their work's done an' their food's packed away for the winter," Dad said. He took his eyes from a tall oak tree and handed Henry a peck basket. "We must do the same. The Good Lord provided us with a wonderful crop this year an' we must take advantage of it. There will be plenty of cannin' and storin' of food for us, too, before winter sets in."

Dad removed his straw hat from his head and walked to the pump beside the barn. Pumping the handle until the icy water flowed in a thick stream he bent down and splashed his face. Pulling his handkerchief from his back pocket, he wiped his face and then the lining inside his hat. "Right now you boys need t' be like those squirrels. There's a lot of pickin' and snappin' t' do before your mom an' the girls can get t' cannin' the crops." He took his straw hat and waved it at Henry and Robert. "Go on now! What are you waitin' for? Get the other boys an' get started on those beans."

"Sure thing, Dad!" Henry and Robert turned from Dad and began calling Eddie and me as they headed toward the field of beans.

"Call Wesley, too," Dad said. "He's old enough now t' know the difference between a bean an' a weed."

All morning we picked string beans, yellow and green. When our baskets were full we carried them to the house where we sat on the side porch and snapped until our fingers became tired and stiff. Then, returning to the garden, we picked more.

"I'm gettin' kinda tired of pickin' beans," Eddie complained. "I think my fingers are gonna turn into beans. In fact, I've seen so many beans I'll prob'ly dream about beans the rest of my life."

"Me, too!" Robert said. "I'll be glad when we start pickin' somethin' different."

That's when Dad came up behind us. "Are you gonna be men or little sissies when you grow up?" he asked. Then he started bragging about the Boys' Home. "Why sometimes, at the Home, we rose long before the sun an' never left the fields till sundown. An' sometimes I walked behind a horse with its reins over my shoulder an' a plow in my hands for hours on end. An' I wasn't no bigger than Carl is t'day. You talk about hard work! My hands were nothin' but calluses! An' you should have seen the fields! We had fields an' fields of corn an' potatoes, cabbage, turnips an' peas. It seemed as far as your eyes could see there were fields of vegetables.

"Mind you, now," he spoke on, "there were eighty of us boys t' care for the crops. But we raised all our own food. An' I can honestly tell ya t'day, I'm glad we did. It taught me a lesson I'll never forget. When the Good Lord gives you somethin' like this earth of ours, you'd better use it wisely an' make the most of it, 'cause if you don't, He might just take it away from you an' give it t' someone who will."

Each of us sheepishly watched Dad as his eyes glistened with pride. We had heard the same story many times before. And each of us knew, if time allowed, Dad would have told of the fun he had at the Home, too. Instead, he just turned and walked away and said, "Don't keep your mom an' the girls waitin' forever, boys."

When the beans were completely snapped and washed, Mom, Esther and Roberta filled large copper kettles with the freshly snapped beans, poured water over them and cooked the beans on the old wood stove until they became sweet and tender. Then, draining the water into the sink, Mom poked the beans into quart jars and added a little more water.

Next, Esther and Roberta screwed the lids on top, placed the jars into another large kettle with water, and set them on the stove to cook for nearly two hours. When the two hours were up, Mom removed the beans from the kettle and set the scalding jars on the kitchen floor to cool. After a few minutes passed, each of the lids 'popped' and Mom said, "Another jar finished and ready for the pantry."

In the following days, the beets were picked, then the carrots, and finally the corn. Each time Mom waited for the 'popping' of the lids and then proudly she placed the jars on the wooden shelves of the cool pantry.

"You know, I'm afraid if we don't watch out, we're going to work ourselves into early graves," she teased as she set the last jar upon the shelf. "I'd say it's about time we all took a break and had some fun." She untied her apron and dropped it on the kitchen table. "Why don't you boys take a break and go fishing. We girls will find some way to relax here in the house. We'll get the rest of the canning done later." She set the copper kettle in the sink to wash. "Go on now!" she said as she shooed us out the door. "I need to think about supper, anyhow."

Behind the outhouse we crossed over the barbed-wire fence and followed our familiar path to the bridge on Anglin' Road. Wild geese began honking above us as they began their annual trip south. Busy beavers had built their dams just around the bend and Yankee Creek no longer rushed with water. Instead of streams rippling over rocks and gurgling around bends, it sat stagnant. A blue haze sat upon the top of the water, stirred only by a gentle autumn breeze and large water spiders that skimmed across the top like tiny ice skaters.

A beaver poked his head through a bramble of thicket in the water and then he was gone. A box turtle poked his head above the stagnant water, stared momentarily, then dipped his head below the water and paddled away.

We baited our hooks with worms, threw our lines into the water, and watched our cork bobbers bob twice at the sudden impact and then rest quietly upon the top of the water. That's when we first saw that strange man. At first we heard the putt-putt sound of his car. As he slowly passed over the bridge he glanced down and spotted us below. Backing his car up, he stopped upon the bridge above and stepped out. Staring down at us he spoke proudly. "Nice day for fishing," he said.

He was a small man, not much taller than Robert. His thin wire glasses pinched his nose at the end. Even though it was the middle of the week and the sweltering heat rose in waves from the earth below, he wore a dark brown suit. His eyes were round and under his nose a trimmed, gray mustache curled at the corners of his lips. Peering over the bridge, he spoke again with an unfriendly smile. "Are you the kids that live in that old house?" he asked, pointing his thumb in the direction of our house.

"Sure. What's it to ya?" Henry answered. He cast his fishing line under the bridge and watched his cork bobber plop and bob in the shade of the bridge.

"Oh, nothing." The stranger propped his foot upon the bridge rail. "Kind of a run-down, old house if you ask me, isn't it? I mean with all you kids."

"It's not a run-down house. We fixed it all up. But that's no business of yours. An' nobody asked ya anyways!" Henry snapped back.

"You call that fixed up? Hardly!" The stranger spoke boldly. "I understand one of your brothers is in a wheelchair."

"Say, mister, what's your point?" Robert asked. He set his bamboo pole back into the water. "It seems t' me you're askin' a lot of questions that don't concern ya."

"Oh, let's just say I'm a concerned citizen. I just believe kids deserve a better break than that in life." With those words the stranger lifted his foot from the bridge railing and slid back into his car. The car door banged and then the car chugged slowly from the bridge and out of sight.

"What did he mean by all those questions?" I inquired of Henry.

Henry picked his bamboo pole out of the water and twirled the string and cork bobber around the top. "I don't know, Carl. Some people don't have the sense they were born with. I wouldn't worry about it none." He shooed some pesky flies from his sweaty head and stared in the direction of the stranger's car as it rumbled down the road. "Come on, let's go home. I don't feel like fishin' no more."

Not a word was said to anyone else about the stranger. It was a secret. But none of us had agreed to keep it a secret. It was just understood that we would not tell anyone about that terrible man.

16 | Dad's Pride

One day when the snows began to fall again, Dad came home from work earlier than usual. He simply walked into the house and dropped his work tools on the kitchen counter. For a few moments he said nothing; he just stood by the kitchen pump and stared into space. But what he was about to announce to Mom was written all over his face. All of us had expected to hear those terrible words soon. Still, each night he had come home and told only of threats of a strike. Now, it was true. T.I.W. was now on strike.

Dad took the pump handle and pumped it up and down and while the icy water poured out he rubbed his hands briskly. "It was not a pretty picture, Lydia," he finally spoke. "Men just simply stopped their machines at nine o'clock an' walked out of the shop. At first, I stood there, not believin' it was really happenin'. Then Harry yelled, 'Let's go, Randall! This is it!' The foremen just stood there an' watched us go. There was nothing they could do." He pulled a kitchen chair near the oak table and sat down to join Mom. "I'm unemployed, Lydia. What do I do now? This thing could go on for a long time."

Mom rose from her chair and went to the kitchen stove. She grabbed the handle of the steaming teakettle and poured the boiling water into a cup she held in her other hand. Reaching into the cupboard for a Lipton's tea bag she spoke. "Perhaps they'll come to their senses soon, Randall. Maybe the fact that you did walk out will hurry the negotiations along, what with Christmas coming along real soon."

"Perhaps," Dad uttered. "But t' hear the men talk, it's gonna be a long strike. They're not anywhere near agreement on any of the issues. I have a funny feelin' it's gonna carry on till next year sometime."

Days and then weeks passed while Dad continued to wait for good news.

Now that the snows had begun to fall, the normal farm work had already been finished. Dad and we boys had already picked the beans, tomatoes, beets, carrots, sweet corn, and potatoes while Mom and the girls had canned all there was to can. After the canning was done we boys jumped into the back of our seven-passenger Plymouth, filled with fresh ears of sweet corn and went to Sharon to sell all that was left. Up and down the streets we went from house to house until all was sold. It was all hard work, but now that the harvesting was done what would Dad do? Occasionally, he drove to town to meet with others to learn of the latest news, but it was never good news. With the unemployment, Dad became depressed and very cross at times. Days went by and he would barely speak. When he did speak, they were usually harsh words that shook the entire house and brought fear to each of us. Everything we did seemed to be futile. If we helped Dad, it usually wasn't enough. If we stayed out of his way, he became angry and complained that he couldn't get anybody to help him around the farm. The food was never cooked to his satisfaction; it was either too hot or too cold. Time and time again Mom tried to comfort Dad and console him, but only in vain.

"Why is Dad so mean an' mad all the time, Mom?" I boldly asked one day.

Mom beckoned me to the kitchen window. "Come here, Carl," she said. She held my hand in hers. "Just take a good look at your dad out back and tell me what you see, Carl."

"I see Dad workin' on his rake at the old well, Mom."

"Yes, but just look at his face, Carl. Now what do you see?"

"He looks real sad 'bout somethin', Mom."

"That's exactly what I mean, Carl." Mom backed slowly away from the window while I continued to stare at Dad prying the long handled pump at the back well. "If you look real close, Carl, everything is written all over your dad's face. You see, Carl, your dad has a lot on his mind. We don't have much money in the house, and with eight children to feed and clothe he's plenty worried."

"We've got plenty of food in the pantry yet, Mom."

"You're absolutely right, Carl. We do have plenty of food. I try to convince your dad of that, but you see, Carl, every man has something inside of him called pride. It's pride that makes a man get up and go to work when he's very sick. It's pride that makes him feel he's a man; the master of his home. It's his whole life. And when that pride is lost or stolen a man becomes weak and depressed. Your dad feels somewhat ashamed that he's not working, Carl. And he's close to losing his pride. We mustn't let him lose it. You and the other kids and I have to help your dad when he needs it. Put up with his swearing and meanness when he's upset. We've got to be tough, Carl. We don't want him to lose that pride. It's going to be hard to do, but we must all do our part. Let's make Dad know that we love him and that we're happy in spite of the way things are. Someday soon he'll be back to work and things will be back to normal."

Holding back her tears, Mom smiled as she ran her fingers through my hair and softly kissed my forehead. "Now, run along, Carl. Why don't you put your coat on and go play with Eddie and Wesley in the snow."

I slipped my boots on and buckled them firmly to my feet. "Maybe Dad can use some help waterin' the cows, Mom. I can play with Eddie and Wesley later."

Mom lifted her apron toward her watery eyes and a warm smile swept across her pretty face. "I've got something in my eye," she said tenderly as she quickly slipped into her bedroom, brushing the tears with the back of her hand.

There was plenty of work for Dad to do around the house, and he never wasted a mere second of his precious time. Each morning he arose early and worked constantly until the sun went down. He picked up odd jobs around town, such as painting and wallpapering. One widowed woman hired him to remodel her kitchen and paid him well. But soon these jobs dwindled to none and Mom feared that Dad would lose his pride. For the next few weeks, Mom watched Dad closely, comforting him, cheering him, and encouraging him constantly.

"You're the best painter around, Randall," Mom told Dad one sleepless night. "Henry said Mrs. Black approached him at school today and said she might have you paint a room or two one of these days."

From our bedrooms above, we could hear Dad pacing his bedroom floor below. He banged his fist hard against the wall. "Don't you know that's just charity, Lydia? Just plain an' simple charity! Everyone in Hartford knows I'm out of work. An' they all know we have eight children. An' one of them is crippled! They all feel sorry for us! Can't you see that, Lydia?"

"They only mean well, Randall," Mom assured Dad.

"Are you blind, woman?" Dad shouted. "Can't you see they all take pride in the fact they were chosen by God Almighty t' come t' our aid?"

Dad paused now and I held my breath hoping he was through. But he wasn't. "I can see them all now," he continued in a softer tone of voice, "parading into church, their buttons poppin' off their chests as they brag about how much good they can do for this poor deprived family of ours."

The silver moon was full. Its beams sparkled off our frosty bedroom windows. I pictured Dad's strong arms resting on the cold windowsill in his bedroom below. "Don't they know I'm a man? I can support my own family!"

"Of course you can, Randall. We'll make out all right. We don't have need for anything. The Good Lord provided us with a good crop this past summer. We've got hundreds of canned foods stored away for the winter. And Lord knows we've got enough coal to last us a good month. We'll do just fine until you get back to work."

"It was a mistake movin' here, Lydia. It's hard for a man t' admit he's wrong, but it was one big mistake! This house has been nothin' but a jinx t' any of us. I swear by the very hairs on my head we'll move back t' Brookfield just as soon as we can!"

Oh, how those words hurt! "A jinx!" Dad had said. Move from Anglin' Road? I didn't want to move from Anglin' Road. I knew it wasn't the prettiest house in town. And I knew we were even thought to be poor by some people. But what did they know? They didn't know about the goose bumps I got all over my body when I first set my feet on this ground. They didn't know that Esther had said it was God's will that we moved here. And they didn't know about Glen's big dream to be in that musical that everyone from miles around bragged about! And they didn't know about the lucky stone that I held up to the stars that night a long time ago and made that wish for Glen to sing in the musical. I could feel the pain go deeply through my whole body. I wanted to cry, but I knew I was too big to do that. Instead, I covered my head with my blankets and plugged my ears. I didn't want to think of leaving Anglin' Road.

When we came home from school the next day Henry's left eye was black and blue and swollen completely shut. When he came into the house Mom just smiled at him, walked to the icebox, and grabbed a small piece of steak. Handing it to Henry she said, "Just place this on your eye. It will take the sting out."

Henry wouldn't explain how he got his black eye, but Robert knew and at the supper table he began to laugh loudly when Dad said, "Well, are you gonna tell us about it or do we have t' guess?"

Henry was still holding the piece of steak on his left eye when he looked to Dad with the other eye. "Someone poked me in the eye while we was playin' basketball after school," he said. "That's all."

Robert laughed louder now. "Why don't ya tell him the truth? It can't hurt no worse than your eye!" he said.

"You'd better be quiet if ya know what's good for ya!" Henry said, switching his good eye to Robert now.

But Robert only laughed harder now and nearly fell from his chair.

"Did you get some good licks in, yourself? I mean did he go home an' put steak on his eye, too?" Dad asked with a chuckle.

Finally, Robert blurted out, "It wasn't a boy! It was a girl who poked him in the eye!"

"A girl?" Dad shouted. *"Do you mean t' tell me a girl gave you a black eye like that? What did she do, hit you with a hammer?"*

Dad put his fork down and began belly laughing. Soon the entire kitchen was filled with laughter and tears of joy.

"No! She didn't hit me with a hammer," Henry said as he, too, began to laugh. "We was arguin' over a disputed call and she just hauled off an' poked me in the eye."

"You didn't hit her back did you?" Dad stopped laughing and looked straight into Henry's eye.

"Of course I didn't! Ya always taught us never t' hit a girl," Henry said. "Besides that, she hit Howard Brown in the eye, too. An' you know Howard. He's bigger than me!"

"My goodness," Dad said as he began to laugh once again, "I'd like t' meet this girl."

"She jis' swung her fis' 'round and poked Henry right in da eye!" Wesley said and swung his arm around, imitating the girl's swing. *"She jis' bopped him a good one!"*

Ha! Ha! Ha! We all laughed until our stomachs ached.

Later, we all gathered around the pot-bellied stove in the living room. Mom set a bowl of walnuts in front of Dad and said, "Why don't you play some songs on your harmonica, Randall. The girls and Glen can sing along." She handed a nutcracker to Robert then took a seat beside Glen. "I sure would like to hear some good music."

"Sure," Dad said. "I could go for some myself." He walked to his and Mom's bedroom and returned with a small red box. He lifted the lid and pulled his harmonica from the box. "My last memory of my dad is right here in this harmonica," he said. "The very last thing I remember him doin', when I was a small boy, was playin' some sad, sad song on this very harmonica." He lifted the harmonica to his mouth and soon the air was filled with a lonely tune called "Down in the Valley". Glen, Esther, and Roberta began singing the sad words of a lonely man asking his girlfriend to send him a letter in care of Birmingham Jail.

I wasn't sure if it was the laughter we had over Henry's black eye or the lonely tune that brought back long ago memories to Dad. However, for the first time in weeks Dad seemed to be himself.

17 | Uncle Clyde Nearly Drowns

Uncle Slim was nearly forty years old and still a bachelor. He was quick-witted and often acted silly for an older man. His hair was beginning to gray above his temples and wrinkles began to form upon his forehead. Like so many other young men who grew up during the Great Depression, Uncle Slim took to drinking the hard stuff, as Grandma called it. And Mom said that was the reason he never married. He hadn't drunk the hard stuff for years, but he still had fun pretending he was drunk around us. Often, he would wobble across a room and deliberately slur his speech and laugh like he had been drinking just to make us laugh.

Everyone loved Uncle Slim and Mom said it was his silliness that brought the joy back to Dad's face. Round and round Uncle Slim would dance a jig for all of us and then, just as quickly, he would act as though he had drunk too much of the hard stuff and tell us he loved us and wanted to marry us. When we all laughed at his silliness, he, too, would laugh at himself, then pick up his guitar and begin singing. Sometimes he would pretend that his finger was stuck in the strings of his guitar and everyone would laugh as he tried desperately to release his finger. The only way he could release his finger, or so it seemed, was to turn his back to us. But each time his finger would become released his guitar would somehow be turned backwards and Uncle Slim would proceed to strum on the back of his guitar while we all laughed till our sides ached.

Sometimes Uncle Slim yodeled, and though it sounded comical to all of us we would cheer and beg for more because Teddy didn't like it. Squatting at the front window, Teddy pointed his nose to the moon and howled like a lost wolf in the faraway woods.

One day Aunt Rose laughed at Uncle Slim and shook her head. "Lord Sakes! You're worse than the kids," she teased.

Uncle Slim stopped his silly antics, slammed his guitar into its case, and mumbled something about never getting married.

When Uncle Slim set his guitar back into its case and snapped the locks into place Grandma asked Mom to call Robert and Ronny into the house. "I know they're playing basketball against the barn, out there, but I want to hear that boy sing before he scoots off to his home. My! My! My! That boy sure can belt a song out!"

When Ronny entered the house, Uncle Slim staggered by him, as though he had been drinking the hard stuff once again. *"Young whippersnapper! Just because you can sing don't mean you're so hot!"* He slurred the words. Then he laughed and whispered into Ronny's ear, "Wait till I get back from the car. I don't want t' miss your singin'."

Standing in front of the kitchen door, Ronny clutched his stocking cap with his tiny hands. His eyes closed tightly. Then he began:

"Besame, Besame Mucho
Each time I cling to your kiss I hear music divine.
Besame, Besame, Mucho
Hold me my darling and say that you'll always be mine.
This joy is something new
My arms enfolding you
Never knew this thrill before
Who ever thought I'd be
Holding you close to me

It's you I adore.
Dearest one, if you should leave me
Each little dream would take wing and my life would be
through
Besame, Besame Mucho
Love me forever and make all my dreams come true."

An unusual quiet fell upon the kitchen when at last Ronny closed his eyes once again, stood tall on his toes, and reached into heaven to borrow angelic notes to finish his song.

From her apron pocket Grandma lifted a tiny handkerchief and brushed a tear while her eyes seemed to search for long ago memories. "I never heard such a voice in all my life!" she said. "Sing one more time, Ronny, and then you may go."

Once again Ronny sang and once again Grandma reached for her tiny handkerchief to dab the happy tears from her watery eyes.

"Okay, Uncle Clyde, it's time to take us sliding on the ice!" Roberta called at the end of Ronny's song. "Please!" She begged. "You promised us!"

"That I did," Uncle Clyde retorted with a chuckle. "But I really didn't come prepared. Just look at my clothes! I'd freeze to death out there!"

"Oh, come on, Uncle Clyde! You can wear one of Dad's coats and hats. Come on, please!" Esther pleaded.

Perhaps it was Esther's pleasing personality. Possibly it was the fact that she tickled Uncle Clyde under his chin and made him laugh. Nevertheless, Uncle Clyde could not resist another minute of our constant pleas and thus he gaily donned Dad's winter apparel and proceeded to lead all of us children to our favorite place to slide near the old wooden bridge.

"Come on out, Uncle Clyde! The ice is solid here. See! We're all standing here and it's holding us. Come on!" Roberta shouted.

Uncle Clyde stood on the bank and pondered the thought. "You're sure it's safe, now?" he asked.

"Of course it is! We wouldn't be standing here if it wasn't safe, would we?" Roberta assured Uncle Clyde.

Uncle Clyde carefully placed his one foot on the ice below and then the other. For a moment he stood there testing the ice. "Okay," he said, "you talked me into it this time." Cautiously, he pushed with one foot and then the other slowly gliding to the center of the creek.

Soon Uncle Clyde was running and sliding from side to side, playing tag with us boys and teasing the girls. First, he tagged me and I fell to the ice, laughing. Then he pulled Esther's braids and tickled Roberta through her coat. Once, he raced across the creek with Robert, but Robert was too fast. On the other side of the creek Robert waited and laughed as Uncle Clyde's wobbly legs shook his entire body until he tumbled to the ice below. What fun it was to see Uncle Clyde fly aimlessly through the air and fall harmlessly to the ice below. But suddenly, without warning, a loud crack rippled across the ice. *Crack! Crack! Crack!* The ice was cracking and Uncle Clyde could see it spreading fast now.

"Hurry to the side, children! Fast now!" he warned us.

Then, just as rapidly as the first crack had come without warning, there were more cracks. But this time the ice became too weak to hold Uncle Clyde. *Splash!* In the middle of the laughing and teasing Uncle Clyde fell through the ice. In an instant the icy water swallowed Uncle Clyde.

"Uncle Clyde! Uncle Clyde!" Roberta cried. *"Where are you?"*

"There he is!" Robert shouted as Uncle Clyde's head suddenly burst through the icy water.

"*I'll help ya, Uncle Clyde! Jist hold on!*" Henry called to Uncle Clyde as he began to move toward the hole in the ice.

"*No! No! Don't any of you come out here! You'll only fall in, too!*" he commanded with quivering voice. "*I'll make it all right by myself. It's no deeper than my neck now. I'll just chip the ice with my fist and work my way to the shore. All of you just stay on the bank. I'll be all right!*"

"Oh, Uncle Clyde! Can't we help somehow?" Roberta cried.

"*I'll be all right!*" Uncle Clyde said as he pounded the ice in front of him and small pieces chipped away, forming a clear path in front of him. His teeth chattered and his lips began to turn blue.

"*Grab hold of that tree, Robert!*" Henry shouted to Robert as he pointed to a small quaking aspen tree on the bank behind us. "*Let's form a human chain an' I'll reach down and grab hold of Uncle Clyde.*"

Robert ran back and grabbed the tree with one hand and held Eddie's hand with the other. Then I held Eddie's hand and Esther held mine. Roberta grabbed hold of Esther's hand and then Ronny's. Ronny then grabbed tightly to Henry's hand. Stretching his body far over the water Henry reached down and grabbed Uncle Clyde's hand.

"*Hold on tight, Uncle Clyde!*" Henry said. Then turning his head, he looked back and shouted to us. "*Pull, everybody! Pull hard now!*"

At the far end of the human chain Robert clung tightly to the tree, pulling until perspiration dripped beneath his stocking cap.

I felt as though both my arms would be ripped from my body, but I squeezed Eddie's and Esther's hands with all my might until, finally, I heard Henry say with a happy voice, "*It's okay now! He's out of the water!*"

Uncle Clyde stood at the edge of the creek dripping with icy water. His face was crimson red, his lips a dark purple. "Look at that, would you! I didn't even lose my glasses." He lifted the glasses from behind his ears and examined them for scratches.

"Thank you, children!" He shivered the words past his quivering lips. "I don't know what I would have done without you!"

"You wouldn't have fallen into the creek without us for one thing, Uncle Clyde!" Eddie laughed with relief.

"Ya better git home fast now, Uncle Clyde. Dad's gonna git real mad, prob'ly, I betcha, 'cause ya got his clothes all wet!" Wesley warned Uncle Clyde with a scowl.

Uncle Clyde began to pull his pants up with his wrists and then burst into laughter. Winking at the rest of us he said, "Well, I guess I'd better hurry home at that, hadn't I children? I sure as heck don't want your dad getting upset over these wet clothes now, do I?"

"Let's go, Uncle Clyde! Hurry now, before you catch a bad cold!" Esther commanded, as she and Roberta latched on to his arms and led him quickly to the house.

At the house, Uncle Clyde quickly dried and changed into his own dry clothes then he propped himself in front of the old wood stove in the kitchen. First, he faced the stove until he could stand the heat no more. Then, he turned his back to the stove until it was toasted. Mom wrapped a blanket around him and as he shivered and turned, and turned and shivered, we children told and retold the story of how Uncle Clyde fell into the frozen creek.

"Well, it's been a fun day as usual," Grandma said as she propped her hands upon the kitchen table, straining to lift her tired body from the hard wooden chair. "I'm afraid it's getting late and Slim must be at work in the morning."

"Yes, it has been a fun day," Aunt Rose replied. "But it is time to get Clyde home before he catches pneumonia."

"But Uncle Clyde! You can't go until you and Dad entertain us with one of your pretty songs," Glen said. "You know how we all look forward to that!"

"By golly, you sure are right, Glen!" Uncle Clyde laughed between shivers. "We certainly wouldn't want to disappoint our loyal fans, now would we, Randall?"

Dad arose from his wooden chair, turned it around, straddled it backwards and propped his feet upon the bottom braces. From his pocket he pulled forth the tiniest harmonica we had ever seen. Teasingly, he plopped it into his mouth until we could barely see it, and suddenly the air was filled with "toe-tappin'" music.

With his blanket still wrapped around him, Uncle Clyde stood in front of the wood stove, smiling and clapping his hands to the beat of the music and soon his high tenor voice was echoing the sweet words of the pretty "Red Wing" across the kitchen walls:

"Oh, the moon shines tonight on pretty Red Wing,
The breeze is sighing and night birds crying
Far, far beneath the stars my love is sleeping
And Red Wing's weeping her life away…"

That evening, as we gathered around the kitchen table, there was a special kind of happiness that filled the air—a happiness that we hadn't seen in Dad in a long time.

"You know, Lydia, we sure don't have much money, but did you ever notice where everybody goes for the finer things in life?" But before Mom could answer, Dad continued. "They come here, Lydia!" He proclaimed proudly. "That's where they go! I swear, Lydia, we've got somethin' here, in this dilapidated, old place that millionaires' money can't buy. I don't know just what it is, Lydia. But there's somethin' here that tells a man he's a man! There's somethin' here that sets one's soul on fire!" He lifted himself from his chair, walked to the kitchen window, and pulled out his tiny harmonica.

Soon the kitchen was filled with songs of long-ago memories as Dad's eyes glistened with pride. He stopped playing the harmonica momentarily and looked back to Mom. "Do you know what I mean, Lydia?"

As the pale moonlight drifted through the kitchen window, Mom nodded her head. For the first time in a long time there was a sparkle in her pretty brown eyes. "Yes, Randall, I know what you mean. I know exactly what you mean," she said.

18 | Christmas Preparations

"I remember a Christmas a long time ago," Mom said as we sat in the living room cracking walnuts. She beamed a pretty smile and her eyes glistened of long ago memories. "I came from a large family, too, you'll recall. There was Uncle Slim, Aunt Martha, Uncle Ralph, Aunt Gloria, Uncle George and me. I'm not saying we were as wild as you kids, but we did have our fun, especially at Christmas.

"Well, one time Uncle Slim got this horrible looking shirt for Christmas. Lord sakes! I don't know where Santa found that thing." She started to laugh and soon we all laughed with her. "Anyway, it was blue and white stripped and it had two pockets, one on each side of the chest with black buttons. The collar and cuffs were white. I guess it looked more like something some rich, spoiled brat would wear, certainly not Uncle Slim!

"Well, we never thought much about it after Christmas, but the next Christmas Uncle Ralph opened up a package and low and behold Uncle Slim had given the shirt to him for Christmas! We had a good laugh over that one. Then the next year Uncle George got the same shirt. Nobody ever wore the shirt. It was still in its plastic cover.

"Years went by and we never saw nor talked about that shirt. Then one Christmas Uncle Slim received the same shirt!" Mom began to laugh again. "The following Christmas Uncle Slim wore the shirt and then passed it on to Uncle George again the next

Christmas." Mom shook her head and plopped the meat of a walnut into her mouth while we laughed louder. "It's hard to believe something that dumb could brighten our Christmases so much."

"I wouldn't be surprised to see Uncle Slim wearin' that same shirt this Christmas. That's somethin' he would do," Glen said.

"Maybe you'll be lucky and get it this year, Glen," Robert teased.

"Well, I guess I'd better check the furnace," Dad said when the laughter stopped. He rose from the sofa chair and left for the cellar. "When I get back we'll go get our tree, boys."

Dad stood in the cellar and took stock of the coal pile. For a long time he stared at the coal. Then he turned and climbed the steps to the kitchen above. He walked to the sink and pumped some water into the basin below. He scrubbed his hands, took the towel hanging on the counter, and as he dried his hands he walked to the rear window and stared at the snow swirling around the outside pump.

"Better tell those boys t' get ready t' go get our tree, Lydia," Dad said. "Looks like that snow's not gonna let up any. No tellin' how long it will take t' pick the right tree out."

Mom reached into the cupboard beside the stove, pulled a box of Morton's salt out, and set it on the table. It was also time to bake the pies and make the favorite dish for Christmas, homemade noodles. She said nothing, but stepped to the door of Glen's bedroom and waved to let us know it was time to go.

"Before you know, it will be Christmas an' the whole gang of relatives and friends will be knockin' on our door," Dad said. He went to a hook in the pantry and pulled his winter coat down. He grabbed his boots, slipped them on, and stood beside the kitchen door.

"Yes, and I've got to get everything ready for tomorrow's pie baking, ham baking, and noodle blending before all that happens,"

Mom said. She opened the cupboard door once more and pulled a can of baking powder.

"If you're goin' with me, boys, you'd better pile into that Plymouth right now," Dad said, as he kissed Mom good-bye, and slammed the kitchen door behind him. "If we don't git a move on it soon, Santa just might be here before we git back!"

I didn't believe Dad when he said Santa would beat us back. But Dad was real particular about which tree he wanted and I found myself wondering if maybe he was right. Round and round, Dad went from tree to tree. If he liked the tree he tied a red bow at the top. Then he moved on to another tree. He looked at that tree, rubbed his chin, shook the snow off the top, and then he tied another red bow at the top of the tree.

Finally, Dad selected the perfect tree! And before we knew it, we were driving up our driveway with the most beautiful tree in the whole, wide world sitting on top of our Plymouth.

"It's a pretty tree, Dad!" Wesley hollered from the side porch, as Dad stepped on the brakes and parked the Plymouth beside the house.

The icy wind whistled across the tree and the sweet scent of fresh pinesap tickled Mom's nose as she stood beside Wesley, Esther, and Roberta. She took a deep breath, buttoned her coat around her neck and shivered. "It's beautiful, Randall! Just beautiful!" she said.

"Well, we could have been here a lot earlier if these kids hadn't kept changin' my mind." He untied the tree from the car and set it firmly to the ground. "Every time I picked a tree out, wouldn't you just know it, one of the boys would say, 'No, Dad. That's not good enough!' I swear they're a hard crew t' work with."

Mom smiled and shook her head. "If they did, it's because you trained them well," she said.

Dad shook the snow off the tree and pushed it toward Henry. "Put the tree in the shed, Henry. Tomorrow is Christmas Eve an' that's when we'll put it up. Uncle Robert an' Aunt Rachel are comin', as they did last year, t' watch me decorate the tree an' we won't place an ornament on the tree till they arrive."

"Ah, Dad! Can't we just set the tree in the house tonight? We don't have to decorate it," Roberta pleaded from the side porch.

"Now you know better than that, Roberta. Dad never puts his trees up before Christmas Eve. I think you can wait one more day," Mom reminded Roberta. "It's more fun if you wait until then anyhow."

"You're so right, Lydia," Dad said. "You'll appreciate it much more if you can just wait one more day. At the Home we never put our tree up till Christmas Eve an' believe me, on Christmas mornin' everythin' seemed new an' beautiful. We never had a moment t' get tired of it. We appreciated every minute of it an' I'm sure you always will, too. Besides that, Uncle Robert an' Aunt Rachel would be mighty hurt if we didn't wait for them."

The day before Christmas, Mom rose very early for she must begin her annual pumpkin pie baking festivities. There was much to do and so little time. But Mom would have it no other way. To begin any earlier would have taken the excitement out of Christmas. Slipping on her long winter coat, she sleepily trudged the cellar steps and stoked the furnace as she did every cold morning. Then, stuffing some old newspapers and kindling into the kitchen stove, she lit a match to the newspapers and watched cautiously as the colorful sparks spread from the paper to the splinters of wood. The thin splinters snapped and crackled while blue sparks turned to golden flames. Slowly, Mom added heavier pieces of wood and small chunks of coal. Now the golden flames danced and sparkled, and cracked and popped. Puffs of black smoke rose from the coal and then the fire was all aglow.

Gently, Mom lifted a sack of flour from under the kitchen sink and set it on the long kitchen table. From the icebox, she pulled nearly three dozen eggs and a gallon of fresh milk. Finally, from the pantry, Mom brought five jars of golden homegrown pumpkin. The annual festivity of making Christmas pies had begun.

Mom kneaded a large bowl of dough, plopped it on the table and began rolling the large ball until it became flat and spread across the kitchen table. Roberta and Esther buttered the fifteen pie plates and while Mom mixed the pumpkin pie ingredients they carefully laid the dough across each plate and carved the extra dough from around its rim. Pressing their thumbs upon the dough at the rims of the plates, they made a pattern of thumb marks around the rims of each pie plate.

Soon, the entire house filled with the sweet aroma of pumpkin pies. When the pies were finished, Mom set them on the kitchen shelf and began to mix more dough. This time she spread the dough across the entire table, sprinkled flour on top, and then sliced the dough into long thin pieces.

When the chicken broth was cooked just right, Mom began dropping the long noodles into the broth boiling on the wood stove. I sucked in the sweet aroma of pumpkin pies and home-made noodles until my head became dizzy and light. "I hope Santa brings me a nice hot bowl of homemade noodles, Mom. That's all I ask for."

"Well, I doubt if he'll bring you much more than that." Mom laughed and put the lid over the steaming pan of noodles. "But I do think that can be arranged."

In the evening the excitement began to rise. Mom pushed Glen into the living room while Esther and Roberta scrambled for the davenport. Robert, Eddie, Wesley, and I plopped ourselves in the middle of the floor, careful not to be in Dad's way. Soon, Uncle

Robert and Aunt Rachel would arrive and Dad would begin placing the colorful antique bulbs on the Christmas tree.

"The sweetest aroma this side of heaven!" Dad boasted as he nailed two flat boards across the base of the tree for support. He lifted his nose to the air and took a deep breath. "What more could a soul ask for than the sweet savory smell of freshly baked pumpkin pies, homemade noodles, an' fresh pinesap tricklin' down the most beautiful Christmas tree in the whole wide world!"

Dad was right. There was never anything that smelled so sweet and wonderful as Mom's pumpkin pies, homemade noodles, and fresh pinesap trickling down the most beautiful Christmas tree in the whole world! I closed my eyes, took a deep breath, and dreamed of Christmas morning.

"They're here!" Henry called from the kitchen. "Uncle Robert an' Aunt Rachel are here!"

Mom looked at the alarm clock resting on the Philco radio. "Land sakes! Just look at that! Uncle Robert said they would be here at six o'clock and it's not a second past six."

Upon entering the side door, Uncle Robert handed Roberta a bag of hardtack candy. He smiled and rubbed her head. Looking to Henry, Uncle Robert spoke softly. "Now, if you'll just take our raps, young man, we'll hurry into the living room so as to not delay your dad one second more." He handed his coat to Henry. Then, as usual, he assisted Aunt Rachel in removing hers and laid it over Henry's outreaching arms.

Uncle Robert was really Mom's uncle, so that made him our great-uncle. His hair was thinning now in his old age. But Dad had said Uncle Robert wasn't as old as he looked. He always walked very slowly and deliberately, as though the next step might be a dangerous one. But that came from being in World War I. Mom said Uncle Robert had seen plenty of action in the war and when it was over he was never the same. When he was younger he was very spry and active.

"He's a fine Christian," Mom said of Uncle Robert. "You'll never hear him say a bad word about anybody."

Now, as he moved slowly to the living room, Uncle Robert took hold of Aunt Rachel's arm and the two of them greeted Dad at the living room door.

"Welcome, Uncle Robert! An' how are you, Aunt Rachel?" Dad greeted them with a handshake that would have stung our hands. "Move over an' let your aunt an' uncle sit on the davenport, girls," Dad said to Esther and Roberta, who were already seated comfortably.

Carefully, Uncle Robert eased Aunt Rachel to the seat below and then took his seat next to her while Dad prepared to decorate the Christmas tree.

Aunt Rachel's white hair glistened under the kerosene lamp and though she was nearly Uncle Robert's age, her face was soft and wrinkle free. There was youth in her old eyes that told of many good days. Her eyes sparkled with a twinkle and Mom said it was a sure sign that in her younger days she surely had broken many young hearts.

Barely a word was spoken now as Dad opened the trunk and unwrapped box upon box of antique Christmas bulbs. Some were bulbs that hung on the trees at the Home. Others were nearly fifty years old, Dad had said. They were his father's before him. There were colorful birds and little bells. There were red bulbs, and blue bulbs, and shiny bulbs, and dull bulbs. But each bulb told a story of its own. And each was remembered from the years before. Beneath the tree, Dad would set the beautiful wax manger with baby Jesus and Mary and Joseph. And once again, I would set my eyes upon that scene and picture myself there on that glorious day when Jesus was born!

First, Dad unwrapped a beautiful angel, stood on a chair, and placed it at the tip of the tree. Her scepter touched the eight-foot ceiling exactly as it did one year ago in Brookfield. Then, one by one, he attached the hooks to the rosy red bulbs, the sparkling silver bulbs, and the frosted blue bulbs and carefully placed them on the tree. The kerosene lamp flickered with a gentle breeze and colorful bulbs twinkled like heavenly stars.

Oh, how I loved those bulbs! Each bulb held a secret of its own. I gazed into a shiny red bulb and laughed at the reflection of my face as it wrapped around the bulb and distorted my face until I looked like a chipmunk filling his cheeks with acorns. I smiled and laughed until I shook and roared like Santa himself. Then my laughter turned to thoughts: thoughts of happy memories as the twinkling bulbs began to unfold their hidden secrets and I became entranced by their hypnotic spell. I thought of happy things and happy times. Everything in the world that was good and every good feeling in the world seemed to flow through my mind and wash away all the bad times and unhappiness the world had ever held.

It was such a beautiful tree! And I had promised myself that I would not let the fact that there would be no electric bulbs to sparkle through the tunnels of angel hair distract me from the real beauty of Christmas.

But soon I was stirred from my deep thoughts by the sound of Mom's soft voice and I turned just in time to hear her speak. "Your dad's been waiting a long time to surprise you kids this Christmas."

"What is it, Mom?" We all pleaded. "Please tell us!"

"Now, just you wait! You'll find out soon enough," Mom assured us. "You must be patient!"

From the large trunk, Dad pulled a long wire that resembled a string of Christmas lights, for it possessed a number of small sockets that were spaced evenly along the wire. Then, opening a smaller box, Dad began pulling tiny, colored, flashlight bulbs from the box. One at a time he screwed them into the sockets on the long wire. Each bulb had been hand painted a different color. Some were red and some were blue. Some were green and others were yellow.

Could this be the secret that Mom had told us about? What good would painted flashlight bulbs do without electricity? How could simple flashlight bulbs light up on a Christmas tree?

Not a word was spoken now as Dad continued to screw the bulbs in place. With the last bulb placed in its socket, Dad wound the string of lights around the tree, pushed them into their proper places upon the limbs of the tree, and quickly left the room, leaving us to wonder what might come next.

Soon, Dad returned with another box. This box was much larger than the others and seemed to be very heavy.

"Now, everyone, close your eyes!" Dad commanded as he set the heavy box directly under the tree. "In just a moment you will see a feat of magic never before seen by human eyes. Keep your eyes closed, now!"

I squeezed my eyes very tight and covered them with the palms of my hands. I wanted to peek and see just what mysteries lay in the heavy box, but I knew if I did it might break the magical spell Dad had prepared. So, all the tighter I squeezed.

"Okay! You can open your eyes, now!" Dad announced. He stepped back from the tree and smiled proudly.

"Oooooooo!" Roberta exclaimed, while her round, green eyes sparkled. "It's just beautiful, Dad!"

"I can't believe it!" Esther gasped. "How can it be?"

There, in front of our very eyes, stood the most beautiful Christmas tree in the whole wide world! Each tiny flashlight bulb had come alive and was now casting brilliant red, blue, green, and yellow beams that seemed to dance around the tree.

"Well, I never!" Uncle Robert whispered to Aunt Rachel and Aunt Rachel just shook her head in disbelief.

"Golly!" Wesley murmured under his breath.

"It's so pretty, Dad!" I said and rubbed my eyes to make sure I wasn't just dreaming.

"How in the world do they light up, Dad?" Glen asked.

Dad's eyes gleamed with pride now. He tucked his shirt into his pants and said, "Well, it really ain't very difficult, Glen. There's a car battery in that box I just brought in. With a few minor adjustments, I just attached these lights t' the car battery. That's all there is to it."

"You make it sound so simple, Randall. It simply amazes me how you come up with all these ideas!" Uncle Robert declared.

"Well, nevertheless, the tree still needs some more decorations. Just wait till the icicles an' angel hair are on. Besides, this room has t' be decorated, too. Here, Henry," Dad said, tossing some red and green crepe paper to Henry. "You kids can start decoratin' the room while I continue with the tree."

Henry held one end of each roll while I took the other through the middle of the room to the opposite corner. Then, twisting the red and green crepe paper together, Henry taped each end to the corners of the ceiling. Robert and Eddie did the same to the other corners, but Dad had to tape the crepe paper above the tree for fear Robert would knock the tree over.

Then, Esther and Roberta took a long red decoration that looked like a large red boot, opened it until it took the shape of a silver bell, and hung it in the center of the room where the red and green crepe paper crossed.

Aunt Rachel lifted her tired body from the davenport. "It's been a wonderful evening, Lydia," she said. "Robert and I enjoy coming here so much. There's so much fun and happiness here.

But it is getting late and we must go. And, Randall, you certainly do decorate the prettiest trees I've ever seen!"

"Well, thank you, Aunt Rachel. An' thanks for comin'. It wouldn't be Christmas Eve without you an' Uncle Robert." He helped her with her coat and spoke for a moment with Uncle Robert.

"Please drive carefully, now," Mom said at the kitchen door. "It's starting to snow again. And please take this pie as a Christmas gift." Mom held the pie out to Aunt Rachel and Aunt Rachel's eyes grew larger.

"Well, for heaven's sake, Lydia!" Aunt Rachel said shamefully. "We've already been blessed more than we deserve. Just being here with you and your family is all we need to make our Christmas."

"Good night, children!" Uncle Robert called from the side porch.

"Good night, Aunt Rachel! Good night Uncle Robert!" We all returned.

"I think they really enjoyed themselves, Randall," Mom said, waving good-bye from the kitchen window.

"I'm sure they did, Lydia. They're wonderful people. I know I enjoy havin' them 'round." Dad pulled himself from the kitchen window and holding Mom's hand he led her to the living room where, once again, we children had assembled ourselves in front of the Christmas tree.

"Well, it's been a long night, children. I'm afraid it's gittin' rather late. It's time t' climb the wooden steps t' dreamland," Dad said.

"Can't we just sit around the tree for one more minute, Dad?" Robert begged. "Jist for a minute, please?"

"Can we Dad? We'll go right t' bed as soon as the minute is up," Henry pleaded.

"Okay," Dad consented. "Just one minute. An' then it's off t' bed with all of you."

Dad slid his hand from Mom's and stepped to the tree. Gently, he lifted a green bulb from its present branch and moved it to another. "Now, that looks a little better, doesn't it?" The brilliant reds, blues, greens, and yellows danced and flickered with the waves of the kerosene lamp. The sweet aroma of pumpkin pies and homemade noodles drifted into the living room.

"I think it's bedtime, children," Mom said. "It's getting late. And you know Santa Claus won't come until you're all in bed and sound asleep. Let's go now! Up those steps!"

And so, two by two, we scampered up the steps to call it a day.

19 | Reindeer on the Roof

I kicked my shoes under the bed then quickly scrambled under the thick, warm quilts. "Do ya think we'll get much for Christmas this year?" I asked. My voice quivered and as the words slipped past my shivering lips it almost sounded as though I were laughing.

"I don't think so," Robert sighed. "Ya know what Mom said. She told us not t' expect too much this year." Simultaneously, with the last thump of his shoe rolling across the middle of the floor, he braced his one hand on the foot of the bed and hurled himself across the bed rail landing comfortably upon the soft quilts. In a moment, he too, squirmed under the warm covers, shaking the last tinge of cold from his frozen body.

"Yeah, but maybe she was jist sayin' that so we wouldn't expect as much as we get," Eddie chimed in from the other bed.

"Well, I wouldn't expect too much anyway, you guys," Esther added from the small bedroom. "Dad's not working, you know. And I happen to know that Mom and Dad don't have much money."

"I think we have a lot to be thankful for anyway, you guys," Roberta said, offering her opinion. "Even if we don't get anything we're doing pretty well for ourselves. We've got nice clothes to wear, even if some of them are hand-me-downs, we're pretty healthy, and we have a lot of fun around here. I think that's all that really counts."

"Yeah, an' our Chris'mas tree is really nice!" Wesley added. His voice was muffled from deep under the covers.

"You know, I was just thinkin' 'bout that black man who came last summer and picked up our ol' clothes. Remember how happy he was t' get Dad's ol' jacket?" I asked. "Remember how he climbed on top of his truck and dug through the stack of clothes till he found that ol' jacket?"

"Yeah! I sure do remember that," Eddie interrupted. "He slipped his own jacket off an' threw it in the pile an' put Dad's on!"

"And remember when he found the dime in Dad's pocket? He wouldn't even keep it!" I declared. "He jist flipped it down t' Robert an' jumped off the truck just smilin' an' whistlin'. Boy, I'll bet his kids don't git nothin' for Christmas."

"You mean 'anything', Carl, not 'nothing'!" Roberta corrected me. "To say don't and nothing in the same sentence is to use double negatives and one just cancels the other out. So what you're really saying is just the opposite of what you mean."

"Oh, for Pete's sake! Who really cares what cancels what out?" Henry retorted angrily. "As long as we know what he means what difference does it make?"

"It makes a lot of difference if you want to become educated!" Roberta snapped back.

"Well, maybe somebody ought t' cancel you out!"

"Makes no mind," Esther squeezed in. "I'll bet he won't even have a Christmas tree."

"I wonder 'bout Bert Becker," I said. "What kind of Christmas can he have? He's all alone out there in the woods. Maybe we could take him somethin' for Chrismas."

"That's a great idea," Robert added. "But what could we give him?"

"It would be great to take him some of our dinner. But the only thing is, we don't know where he lives. And we don't know if he'd even accept us," Esther said. She paused momentarily. Then, pulling the covers tightly around her neck she added, "You know, I really won't mind if I don't get anything this year. I just hope that Mom and Dad don't feel bad because they can't afford much."

Henry smirked and held his laughter in. "What's all this silly talk 'bout, anyways? You ain't done nothin' 'round here all year. You'll be lucky if Mom and Dad even let ya come downstairs an' watch me open my gifts tomorrow."

"Oh, that's real funny, Henry!" Roberta snapped with a scowl. "Like you really work hard!"

"Of course I do! I milk Daisy Mae, don't I?"

Esther's ears surely turned hot with anger because I heard her snarl from under her covers. "Big deal! You wouldn't know what to do if you had to do real work like mopping floors and doing dishes."

"Now just what's so hard 'bout doin' dishes?" Robert joined in. "Cleanin' the barn out, an' farmin', an' stuff like that's a lot harder than doin' the dishes!"

"Well, how come you always complain when Mom makes you do the dishes then?"

"'Cause that's girls' work. Ya think I want t' go t' school with lily white hands an' have everyone make fun of me?"

Triumphantly, Henry snickered at the argument he had insti- gated. "Your hands look lily white anyways 'cause ya don't do nothin' round here t' make them tough like mine," he teased.

It was a setup and I knew it now. How foolish Robert must have felt to fall into one of Henry's traps again. How ridiculous we all felt for allowing Henry to incite us so on Christmas Eve! Grasping his pillow firmly, Robert flung it hard in the direction of Henry. In a moment a barrage of pillows filled the night air. Back and forth the pillows flew and the clamor rose steadily higher. In the next few moments the laughter rang and pillows continued to fly. But, somehow, above it all, the wisdom of Roberta's pleading words seemed to reach our merciless hearts as she reminded us to quiet down, "… or Dad's going to come up and take his belt to all of us!"

"I'm fursty anyhow!" Wesley panted as he hopped out of bed and threatened to go downstairs. His bare feet hit the cold floor and sent a shiver up to his spine. He shook like a wet dog and started toward the steps.

"Nothin' doin', young man!" Henry sang out as he latched on to Wesley's' ankle and wrestled him to the floor. "You know the Christmas rules 'round here. *Nobody* goes downstairs on Christmas Eve, 'ceptin' they're real sick an' maybe *dyin' or somethin'.*"

Wesley kicked his leg loose of Henry's strong hold. "Well, I'm fursty!" He grumbled. "I'm goin' in da udder room an' call down t' Mom."

Stumbling in the dark, Wesley inched his way slowly to the large, empty room next to the boys' bedroom. Clinging to the walls, he was guided to an eight-inch hole in the floor, as a dim light burst through from the room below. Years ago the hole had been cut into the floor so stovepipe could fit through it and then out the roof. But this was never put into effect so instead of being a channel for stovepipe, it more appropriately became a direct means of communication to anyone in Glen's bedroom directly below. And though the heat flowing through the hole was far from sufficient, its presence sent a warm shiver through Wesley's bones as he knelt to the frigid floor and stuck his face to the hole. "Hello, down dere!" he called.

But there was no answer.

"'Hello,'" I said, 'down dere!' Is dere anyone livin' down dere?"

"What do you want?" a deep baritone voice replied from below.

"Is dat you, Glen?" Wesley asked suspiciously.

"Well, if it isn't me just who would it be in my bed?" Glen snapped. His eyes took a questionable look to the hole in the ceiling above.

"Hey, Glen, tell Mom if I can get up!"

"Tell Mom what?" Glen asked, obviously uncertain that he had heard Wesley correctly.

"I'm fursty, Glen! Tell Mom if I can get up!"

Certain now that he had heard Wesley correctly, Glen shook his head in disbelief. "Mom's busy. And even if she wasn't I wouldn't *tell her* if you can get up! You know the rules for Christmas Eve, so you'd better get back to bed before I *tell her* if she can *paddle you!*"

"Ah, shucks!" Wesley grumbled, lifting his face from the hole in the floor. "I could die from furst an' nobody'd care. But I 'pose that's 'gainst the Christmas rules, too, dough!"

Carefully, Wesley picked his feet through the pitch-dark room, groping, stumbling, until finally reaching his bed he clumsily crawled over Eddie. *"Ouch! You're steppin' all over me!"* Eddie bellowed. *"You clumsy fool!"*

"Can't help it none!" Wesley protested. "Can't see a blasted thin'."

"Well, ya ought t' know I'd be here! I was here when ya left!"

"Will you two keep it quiet in there?" Esther complained.

"Well, how would ya like it t' be half asleep an' have someone step on your nose?"

But there was no reply to Eddie's question. Esther covered her curly head and cuddled close to Roberta who was fast asleep. Robert and I lay awake with sand-filled eyes and deep yawns that seemed to tap our strength like a wind-up toy, slowly running down. Henry snored loudly and then softly as though on cue. Then, without care to the rest of us his sudden silence went unnoticed. Wesley burrowed beneath the covers, grumbled something to himself, curled into a ball beside Eddie, and finally surrendered to the Christmas rules.

Outside, the moon hid behind some fast moving, gray clouds. The blustery wind whistled as it whipped around the corner of the house, beating a rhythmic patter against the cold windowpanes that only lulled us to a more pleasant sleep. But suddenly, our bedroom became alive with soft tapping sounds and I bolted upright in our bed. My eyes swelled and I held my breath. I knew that sound! Henry had described it well to me before. It was the faint cadence patter of tiny feet upon the roof of the house I had just heard. I paused now and took another deep breath. The cold air sent a sting to my throat, but I dared not cough. Once again the patter of tiny feet echoed throughout the dark room and I prayed it wasn't only my rapid heartbeats.

"Will you quit movin' the covers?" Robert pulled the covers in a disgusted manner and wrapped them firmly around his shoulders.

I lay back in bed, but once again I bolted upright, and once again Robert complained. "There ya go again! Will ya quit pullin' the covers off my back? I'm freezin'!"

"What's going on out there you two?" Esther groaned.

"He keeps pullin' the covers off me!" Robert complained.

"Well, I heard somethin' on the roof!" I half whispered and half yelled excitedly.

"Personally, I don't care what ya heard on the roof! Ya didn't have t' wake up the whole house 'bout it an' freeze me t' death!" Then he snapped the covers around his neck and plopped to the bed below.

"Well, what if it's Santa Claus?" I protested.

Eddie agreed. "It jist might be Santa Claus, 'cause while ya were arguin' I heard it, too!"

"Me, too!" Wesley said.

"Well, it can't be Santa 'cause you can never hear Santa. He's too quiet even for your big ears!" Robert said.

But then the cadence of tiny hoofs on the roof grew louder. Suddenly the dark bedrooms became as silent as a graveyard. Robert and I both sat upright in our bed, too excited to breathe.

"I heard it, too, that time!" Esther finally said, as her excited voice broke the long silence. Suddenly, the patter became more prominent as the tiny feet seemed to dance all over the roof.

"Isn't it exciting?" Roberta said through the dark of the night.

"I told ya!" I cheered. And once again Robert snatched the covers back from me.

"We'd better be quiet or he won't come down the chimney," Eddie suggested.

"Best thing to do is just lay back down and close your eyes," Esther said. "It's just like Eddie said. He won't come into the house until we're all fast asleep."

From a far corner of the boys' bedroom, Henry laughed loudly. *"Ain't it jist wonderful!"* he teased. And the tapping grew louder. *"I can make them dance all over the roof! First, they're over here!"* He laughed louder, now, as he jumped around the room thumping the broom handle against the ceiling. *"Then, they're over here!"*

"Ah! That was just you tappin' on the ceilin'!" I protested. And with the last thump from Henry's broom handle I settled back in bed and pulled the covers to my neck.

Once again, Henry's loud laughter rang throughout the upstairs rooms as he hopped around the room thumping wildly against the ceiling. "I sure fooled ya guys that time!"

"You didn't fool anybody," Roberta assured Henry. "We knew it was you all the time."

"Oh, sure ya did! That's why ya said, *'Isn't it excitin'?'*"

Once again Henry laughed and this time he rolled in his bed and held his stomach. But this time he could have saved his laughter had he known that both sisters refused to listen to any more nonsense. Tucked under their four blankets, Esther and Roberta poked their fingers into their ears and began to softly hum, so as to not hear another word Henry was saying. Eddie and Wesley tossed in their bed and covered their heads. Robert gave a faint sigh and tucked his head under his pillow. I closed my heavy eyes and thought of Christmas morning.

Now and then a proud chuckle broke through the cold, night air as Henry turned in his bed, wallowing in victory. But soon seven tired children were fast asleep, summoning the morning sun to come quickly.

20 | Christmas Day

In the morning there was a mad scramble as we hurriedly dressed and wildly thumped across the wooden floors and down the frozen steps to the door below. Esther pushed the door open until there was a narrow slit between the doorjamb and the door.

One by one we peeked through the crack, gaping at the colorful wrappings under the tree, wondering what splendid gifts each wrapping might contain. We laughed, we giggled, and we teased. Each of us fancied ourselves running wildly across the wood floor, rushing to be the very first at the foot of the tree. Each of us dreamed of being rewarded, far beyond our greatest expectations. But deep in our hearts there was warmth and understanding, for we were well aware how Mom and Dad had struggled earnestly the entire year to simply make ends meet. We knew, too, that Mom and Dad had done without so many things that others had taken for granted, simply to make life more enjoyable for us.

Still, there was a longing we could not explain to burst through the door into that magical world of Christmas, where just the mere sight of the Christmas tree with all its trimmings made one so happy to be alive.

"How much longer do we have to wait, Mom?" Esther called through the narrow slit in the doorway. She pushed the door a smidgen more and once again gazed at the sparkling Christmas tree.

"It'll be at least ten minutes. I've got to get Glen up first," Mom exclaimed. Then she smiled and pushed the door closed, nearly catching Esther's nose. "You'll just have to wait and be patient."

"Ho, boy!" Esther sighed. She folded her arms and leaned against the wall. "Hey! Where's Wesley? Don't tell me he's still sleeping," she inquired, counting noses.

"Naw, he's up," Eddie replied. "He's in the other room above Glen's bedroom."

"What's he doin' in there?" Henry spoke with a puzzled look.

"How should I know? The last time I saw him he was stickin' his nose through the hole in the floor. I guess he thinks he can see the presents from there." Eddie sat down on the steps and began to laugh.

"Are ya kiddin' me?" Robert snickered. "The tree's not in Glen's room! It's clear over here, under our room!"

"Don't tell me 'bout it! I could figure that out. Tell Wesley!"

Roberta shook her head in disbelief and held her hand to her smiling lips. "He'll need long eyeballs to see down that hole and into the next room!" she bantered.

I held my stomach from laughter. "I hope he doesn't get his head caught in the hole!" I laughed louder.

Finally, above the loud clamor, Mom announced that Glen was dressed and seated in front of the tree. Before one could count to three, we children exploded past the door like popcorn bursting in a popper and scrambled around the tree.

How majestic the tree looked with its glittering lights and shining bulbs! Around the base of the tree colorful presents were neatly stacked. And now, as we had expected, angel hair garnished the entire tree with perfect tunnels of glass cobwebs that spun around each light bulb setting the tree aglow with brilliant bursts of dancing colors.

"It's just a little trick the elves taught me," Dad teased when we marveled at such a feat of magic.

Eddie and I plopped ourselves in front of the tree and laughed though we could not tell why. Esther and Roberta took their places on the long davenport, and Robert paused a moment to kneel beside Glen's wheelchair.

When Dad and Mom left the room momentarily, Henry's eyes followed them suspiciously. Looking back to us, he smiled. "There must be some mistake!" he announced, as his fingers seemed to be totaling his presents. "There's only three presents for me! Are Mom and Dad hidin' my other presents t' surprise me later?"

"There's been a mistake all right," Esther was quick to snap back. "You shouldn't have any presents!"

"I don't think that's a very funny joke Henry just pulled," Roberta whispered into Esther's ear, "especially since Mom and Dad feel bad that they couldn't afford any more. And just look at Robert!" She spoke louder now, as Mom and Dad entered the room. "He looks like a dog sniffing out a rabbit the way he's going through those presents!"

Wesley thumped down the steps and into the room carrying one shoe and both socks. Rubbing his sore neck, which had apparently become stiff from peeking through the hole in the upstairs floor, he somberly plopped himself in the middle of the room and proceeded to put his other shoe on. On his lap lay both socks.

"Well, guess who's finally showed up for the party," Henry laughed deliberately.

"Now if that don't take the cake!" Glen roared. "Just what are you gonna do with your socks now that your shoes are on?"

Wesley held both socks at arm's length and dropped his eyes to his cold feet below. "'Tain't funny, ya guys!" He snarled as we all began to laugh. "I could catch pamonia an' ya'd all laugh!"

"Henry laughed louder. "That's not '*pamonia*', goofy! It's '*pee-noomonia!*'"

"*Pee-noomonia?*" Esther squealed with delight. "You're just as goofy as he is. It's pronounced '*noo-monia*'. The 'P' is silent."

"Okay, okay! So what if it is? Things would be a lot better if you were silent!"

Once again Roberta cringed at Henry's ability to slaughter the English language so easily and not even care. However, her ill thoughts of Henry were short lived as she spied Robert under the tree inspecting all the packages like a hound dog sniffing the trail of a wild opossum in the pale moonlight.

"Will you please tell Robert to get his nose out of all those packages, Mom?" she growled. "I don't want him slobbering all over my presents!"

"Don't worry," Robert retaliated, "ya didn't get nothin' anyways!"

"I think you'd better get started, Randall," Mom whispered as she pulled Robert away from the tree.

From the davenport, Roberta's eyes caught Robert's once more. This time her hazel eyes crossed and her tongue erupted from her mouth in such a manner that Robert could only laugh and hope she would freeze that way. However, two seconds later Roberta sat in angelic fashion upon the davenport, her legs crossed, looking every bit like a refined, gently bred debutante of a most aristocratic family while Robert chose to drop the whole issue.

Dad lifted a small, red package from under the tree. "The first present," he said, as he read the small card, "is for Glen." Dad handed the package to Wesley to pass on to Glen. Wesley began to open the package because he thought it was for him.

"Can't you hear well?" Roberta snapped as she reached over and snatched the present from Wesley and handed it to Glen.

"He can't help it if he can't hear well. Ya wouldn't hear well neither if ya had your head stuck in that hole upstairs all mornin'," Henry teased.

"Hurry up and open it, Glen!" Esther said. "We want to see what it is."

Around the room we waited patiently as, carefully, Glen's thin fingers tore the wrappings from the small box. "It's a paint set!" he said as his eyes rose to meet Mom's. "Thanks, Mom! Thanks, Dad! It's just what I'd hoped for!"

A sudden hush fell upon the room as each of us reflected upon Glen's happiness with the simple set of paints.

"Perhaps, now, you can paint those beautiful landscape scenes you draw so well," Mom beamed.

"And maybe he can even sell them," I added with a smile.

"Land sakes, it wouldn't surprise me one bit!" Mom beamed again. "Everyone knows you've got more talent in one finger than most other people do in their entire bodies, what with your singing and ukulele playing, too."

Glen blushed and gratefully said, "Are we gonna sit around and talk about me all day or are we gonna see what everyone else got?"

"You're absolutely right, Glen." Dad laughed aloud and called Wesley's name from another package.

Once again he handed the package to Henry who passed it to Robert, who finally handed it to Wesley. Wesley stared at the package, then back to Dad.

"Well, go ahead and open it! You're allowed to open your own gifts, silly," Glen exclaimed with a chuckle.

In another instant the package was open and Wesley now sported a fine leather holster around his waist while two cowboy pistols whisked in and out. Not aware now of the other gifts still waiting to be passed out, Wesley wandered around the room drawing the pistols quickly from his hips, thwarting any attempt of the bad men of the wicked west to endanger the lives at hand.

One by one, Dad continued to pass the remaining packages to our eager hands. There was a basketball for all of us boys. Each received a brand new fishing pole equipped with the finest reel we had ever seen. There were sweatshirts, too, for each of us boys; each bearing a picture of Roy Rogers or Gene Autry on top of their horses, waving their ten-gallon hats to the world around. There were two songbooks for Glen, while Esther and Roberta each received a pair of new shoes and a diary to keep their daily secrets.

At last, from behind the tree, Mom pulled the final two packages and handed them to Esther and Roberta. "I deliberately saved these two for last," she said. "They're something special for the two of you." She held the presents out to the girls and smiled that same warm smile that meant I love you, though not a word was said. "Well, for goodness sakes, go ahead and open them!" She laughed as the two girls stood with round eyes and open mouths.

As Esther and Roberta's fingers tore quickly through the wrappings, Mom watched anxiously.

"Oh, Mom!" The two girls chorused their excitement, as two long dresses unfolded and draped to the floor. "They're just what we wanted!"

At arm's length, Roberta now fastened her eyes to a dusty blue dress with soft petals and fancy lace that hung daintily around the neck and each arm. Esther's was quite similar in design. Soft petals dotted a mellow pink and around the neck and each arm was the same embroidered lace. Each dress was full length and hung midway between the knees and ankles.

"They're just printed dresses I made from colorful feed sacks your dad brought home from the feed mill, nothing fancy. Still, I thought you two might appreciate them." Mom spoke with an air of humility and love together."

"Oh Mom! They're simply exquisite! We couldn't have asked for any more," said Roberta.

"You must have spent hours on these, Mom. When on earth did you find time to make them?" Esther asked, caressing her dress affectionately as she waited for Mom's reply.

"It's what we adults choose to call, 'moonlighting it,'" Mom boasted, and then proudly smiled. "But now it's time for you two to hurry up those steps and try the dresses on. I can't wait to see if they'll fit all right."

"Okay, Mom!" Roberta gleamed as she kissed Mom on the cheek and darted up the stairs. "We'll be right back in a jiffy."

As the two girls proudly pranced around the room, Mom examined the dresses with a skillful eye. "Perfect!" She proudly beamed. "They couldn't fit any better if I'd had you two beside me the whole time. Now, hurry up and change into your other clothes. Your grandma and Uncle Slim and all the others will be here any minute, now. And we still must mash the potatoes and make gravy."

One by one the cars pulled up the driveway and parked near the barn. Grandma and Uncle Slim were first to arrive. Uncle Slim helped Grandma to the kitchen door then hurried back to get his guitar. Next, Uncle Art and Aunt Martha arrived with their five children; Darlene was the oldest, being six months older than me, Jewell was Wesley's age, nearly six years old now, and Joel was only four. Sandy was the youngest of the girls at three years of age, and Lewis was a newborn baby who received more attention than all the others.

Aunt Rose and Uncle Clyde came prepared for ice sliding as each was dressed in the warmest of winter clothes and teased of falling through the ice again. Uncle Jack and Aunt Irene came from far away Mercer, Pennsylvania with their three children; Betty, who was Roberta's age, young Jack, who was my age, and

Joel who was Wesley's age. Aunt Rachel and Uncle Robert came after supper. And Ronny Santana came later to share in the fun and excitement.

Soon the house was filled with merriment and hearts were lifted as friends and relatives feasted on baked chicken, homemade noodles, and Mom's delicious pumpkin pies. There was singing, dancing, and laughter as everyone gathered around the Christmas tree and Uncle Slim strummed his guitar.

Finally, Aunt Rose summoned the attention of everyone as she said, "I'd like everyone to see this special gift that Clyde and I bought Henry. It's just a little gift that we thought you deserve for all the work you've been doing to help your mom and dad, Henry," she said, now addressing Henry.

Proudly, Henry rose from the floor where he had been squatting uncomfortably in front of the tree. He smiled and lifted his nose to Esther and Roberta. "See! They know who really works 'round here," he whispered. Turning to Aunt Rose he gratefully accepted the heavy box she held and then boasted loudly, "There's no doubt I deserve this more than anyone else!"

All eyes were on Henry, now, as he anxiously tore open the package. Suddenly, his face became crimson red.

"Well, show them what it is!" Uncle Clyde teased.

Henry reached into the box and lifted a large lump of coal.

"You sure do 'zerve it more'n anyone else!" Wesley squealed and then smiled so all could see that he was missing his two front teeth. Once again laughter filled the room.

"It's time to be merry!" Uncle Clyde shouted above the laughter. And quickly he lifted Grandma from the davenport and swept her feeble body around the room as Uncle Slim began strumming his guitar. Dad reached into his pocket and pulled his harmonica out. He stepped to Uncle Slim's side and began to harmonize to Uncle Slim's guitar. Around the room others began slapping their knees and stamping their feet. Round and round the young girls swirled their dresses and men and boys kicked their heels.

It was our first Christmas on Anglin' Road and what a wonderful time we all had. But all too soon the hours melted away. And one by one the cars that once crowded our driveway were now slowly pulling away.

Standing in front of the kitchen window, Mom and Dad waved farewell to each of the cars as friends and relatives drove down the long driveway and onto Anglin' Road. Dad put his arm around Mom's shoulder and pulled her near while I watched with admiration. There was a special twinkle in their eyes now. And their faces seemed to radiate as they never had before. But how could they be so happy when they knew very well there were no expensive gifts for either of them, only the small tokens we children had mustered together with our small change. But they had pinched every penny they could put together to make this a happy occasion for everyone else - never expecting a solitary gift for themselves.

I thought of Mom and how hard she must have worked all her life and how little she seemed to get in return. How pretty she would have looked today if she could have just received that pretty coat she was staring at in the catalogue one day! How happy Dad would be if he could only have that harrow he had hoped to buy before spring!

Dad took an apple from the kitchen table and caught me staring into space. "What's the matter with you?" he asked as he rubbed my head. "Are you forgettin' that this is a day t' be happy?"

"Oh, no, Dad! I could never do that. I guess I'm jist a little sleepy, that's all."

"Well, I guess we all are by now," Dad said. He took another bite of his apple and departed to join the others in the living room, beside the tree.

"Mom," I said as we stood alone in the kitchen, "you an' Dad didn't git anythin' for Christmas, did ya?"

"What?" Mom asked with a surprised look upon her face. "Now, what makes you think a foolish thing like that?" she answered with a pretty smile. The kerosene lamp flickered in her slightly graying hair.

"Well, I didn't see you and Dad open any real gifts, Mom."

"Real gifts?" She seemed surprised. She reached down and held my hand in hers. "Well, son, there are some gifts that can never be wrapped and put into boxes."

"There are?"

"Of course there are! They're much too important to be confined to such little things as boxes. Why, they're so big and so wonderful this room can't even hold them!"

"It can't?" I asked in wonder.

"No, Carl, it can't. The gifts I'm talking about are things you can't pick up and hold, or even wear. And there's no price tag big enough to put on them."

"Wow! They must be somethin' real special!" I said in awe.

"That they are, Carl! I'm talking about something called love and happiness, Carl. You see, when your Dad and I know that all you children are happy and healthy, that's the greatest gift we could have. And who could ever deny the wonderful time we all had today! Now, you wouldn't want to spoil all of that for us and have us receive some silly gift that comes in a little box, would you?"

"No, I guess I wouldn't, Mom. I jist like t' see you and Dad happy, that's all."

"Well, then, I guess that takes care of this silly talk, doesn't it?"

Mom smiled and kissed the top of my head. "Let's join the others and celebrate Christmas," she said. "Before you know it Christmas will be all over and you and I will have missed the fun."

I smiled in return. Miss the fun? Never! I would treasure this day forever.

21 | Glen's Illness

Spring planting came and then the hazy days of summer quickly followed. The hot, muggy air was filled with the clinking sounds of hoes and rakes digging lumpy soil, distant voices as we children called to one another across the far fields, and the rumble of Dad's homemade tractor in the fields behind the barn. Dad was back to work now, although Dad said that TIW threatened to move.

Still, the rumble of Dad's tractor, distant laughter, and the clinking of hoes and rakes were music to Mom's ears as she busied herself around the kitchen. However, from the side porch came the most beautiful sounds of all, music! Sometimes it came with the bursting of the golden sun upon the dew-damped earth, and sometimes in the heat of the afternoon. But most of the time it sprang loose in the cool of the evening when all the work was done and Ronny Santana took turns with Glen, Esther, and Roberta performing on the makeshift stage of the side porch.

This November the musical would be held in the Hartford school gymnasium. People would come from miles around to behold the show of all shows! Only the best performers would be invited. The audience would expect nothing less. And the best part was, Glen, Esther, and Roberta had already been accepted, just like I knew they would be. They would be the best singers there! But now there was little time to waste in practicing. "Practice makes perfect!" Glen always reminded Esther and Roberta.

And so, night after night and day after day, between the chores of the day, we could hear the enchanting sounds of sweet voices filling the country air. First, Ronny sang his song. Then Glen, Esther, and Roberta took the stage. Roberta sang soprano and reached the high notes like Ronny. Grandma said she could sing like a sparrow. Esther could sing soprano or alto. But when she sang with Glen and Roberta, Esther always sang alto because it was perfect harmony. "The sweetest music this side of heaven!" Uncle Clyde always boasted.

One evening, the air was extra humid and one could perspire with very little effort. Dad hopped off the Willys tractor, grinned at Uncle Clyde, and slapped him on the back. "Not a bad day's work," he proudly declared. Next, he dusted his overalls and wiped the sweat from his face with his handkerchief while he and Uncle Clyde headed toward the house saying little nothings about the sweltering heat. There was a small gathering in front of the porch, as usual, and on the porch Glen sat erect with Esther standing on one side and Roberta on the other. Underneath Glen's wheelchair, Teddy assumed his favorite position.

Uncle Clyde hitched up his pants with both wrists then cupped his left hand around his ear. A smile swept across his face and nothing could distract him from the stage above. Dad smiled at Uncle Clyde, took his handkerchief from his back pocket, wiped his brow again, and gazed at the trio on the porch.

"Let's hear my favorite!" Uncle Clyde demanded when the trio finished their song. "You know, 'Whispering Hope!'"

"Why not?" Glen smiled as he winked to Esther and Roberta. "It's the one song Mom and Grandma want us to sing in the musical."

Esther looked to Roberta and the two began humming until they agreed upon the same key. Glen softly strummed the ukulele. Then, all together they began:

"Soft as the voice of an angel,
Breathing a lesson unheard,
Hope, with a gentle persuasion,
Whispers her comforting word.
Wait till the darkness is over,
Wait till the tempest is done,
Hope for the sunshine tomorrow,
After the shower is gone.
Whispering Hope, Oh, how welcome thy voice,
Making my heart in its sorrow rejoice.
If, in the dusk of the twilight,
Dim be the region afar,
Will not the deepening darkness
Brighten the glimmering star?
Then, when the night is upon us,
Why should the heart sink away?
When the dark midnight is over,
Watch for the breaking of day,
Whispering Hope, Oh, how welcome thy voice,
Making my heart in its sorrow rejoice."

"Bravo! Bravo!" cried Uncle Clyde. "Doggone, that sure was beautiful! With you three and Liz and Ronny in that musical there won't be any need for any other entertainers!"

"Hush up and leave the kids alone, you ol' fool!" Aunt Rose teased. "Can't you tell they're already gettin' big headed?"

Mom laughed whenever Aunt Rose told Uncle Clyde to hush, but now she detected something in Glen's throat. His face was somewhat paler than normal, and earlier in the day there was a deep cough. However, it was Aunt Rose who swept everyone away, pushing us boys toward the barn, and Dad and Uncle Clyde to the pump beside the house to clean themselves.

Soon the small crowd was dispersed and Mom pushed Glen into the house.

"Take care of that throat, young man, or you'll find yourself in bed," Aunt Rose warned Glen. "You go gettin' sick at a time like this and I'll box your ears in!" There was no laughter in Aunt Rose's voice, she always spoke rough. But inside there was a heart bigger than gold, Mom always said. Even now, Glen knew she was being kind even though her voice didn't say so.

That night I could hear sick sounds downstairs; the sounds of Mom shuffling her feet across the hard floors and into Glen's bedroom. Then, there were tinny noises of metal pans clanging and the familiar sound of the dipper banging inside the water bucket. Finally, I heard the loud, scary coughs from deep down in Glen's chest. Within an hour the sounds repeated themselves. Glen was ill.

In the morning, Teddy became restless and irritable. At first he sat on the porch and snapped angrily at the pesky flies. Then, pacing back and forth across the porch, he waited impatiently for Mom to push Glen to his favorite spot near the railing. Periodically, he rambled down the wooden steps, lapped some water from the fresh rain puddles, and then slowly returned to the porch. His ears hung low and his tail wagged slowly. He pressed his nose against the screen door, hoping to get a glimpse of Glen, and when that failed he slowly curled his red body into a soft ball and rested his weary head on his two front paws. Each time the door creaked Teddy's ears perked up, his tail wagged vigorously, and he faced the screen door in great anticipation. Then, realizing that these, too, were only false hopes, he set his weary head once again on his front paws and with sad eyes, gave a soft whimper.

On Sunday morning, Mom entered Glen's bedroom with a special smile. She cranked Glen's bed to a sitting position and then said, "I heard there's a program on radio that you might like. Aunt

Rose told me about it and said I'd better let you listen to it. She said it will perk you up. And you know Aunt Rose. If we don't give it a try, she'll want to know why." Mom smiled and then turned the radio on and tuned the dial to WPIC in Sharon, Pennsylvania.

Glen gave a half-hearted smile, as though he were thinking of Aunt Rose. Mom then handed him a warm cup of chocolate milk. He wrapped his thin hands around the cup and took a small sip. "Good morning, friends and neighbors!" A gentleman's mellow voice came through the radio. "This is 'Pillow Talk', a program broadcast especially for shut-ins across the western Pennsylvania area. Each Sunday morning we present music just for you to brighten your day and bring a little sunshine into your life. Hello! My name is Larry Vincent and I promise to play music that will lighten your life. Today's first song goes out to Janice Porter from West Middlesex. Janice has been bed ridden for three weeks and anxiously awaits the day she can get out of that bed and get outside. We hope that day comes real soon, Janice. Here's a song especially for you."

Glen listened to the song while Mom studied his face. "It's good that they do this, Mom," Glen said as he handed the cup back to Mom. "I mean I'll bet that means a lot to Janice right now."

"I'm sure it does, Glen." Mom said. "It's nice to know others care." Then Mom reached down and held Glen's hand in hers. Together the two listened to the remainder of the program.

"It seemed to perk him up like no medicine could," Mom told us at the supper table that afternoon. "But when the program was over Glen's sickness seemed to quickly sneak back into his body. His face seemed grayer and his eyes seemed sadder." Mom pulled a tissue from her apron pocket and wiped the tears from her eyes.

"He'll be ok, Mom," Roberta said as she walked around the table and hugged Mom. "He's been through this before."

"I know," Mom said and then attempted to smile. "He'll be just fine. It's just going to take a while."

In the days that followed, Mom would excitedly tell us that Glen's health had reached a plateau. She said it was a sign that he had reached the bottom. Perhaps, now, his health would begin to perk up. But each time he slipped a little lower.

Doctor Higgins came. After checking Glen with his stethoscope he pounded on his weak chest and stuck a long stick he called a tongue depressor on Glen's tongue and told him to say "ah."

"You're a tough man," he said to Glen. "In a short while you'll be back in that wheelchair and back to normal health." Then, packing his instruments into his black satchel, Doctor Higgins bid Glen a pleasant farewell and slipped quietly to the side door. At the side door he hung his sad head low. Wearily shaking his head, he whispered to Mom that Glen was slowly failing.

Each night we could hear the same 'sick' sounds coming from Glen's bedroom below. Occasionally we would hear Glen's deep baritone voice, but never was it harsh - never did he speak an unkind word. Never did he complain or feel sorry for himself.

Each Saturday morning Doctor Higgins returned and each time he followed the same ritual. First, he parked his car beside the side porch, opened the door, patted Teddy's head, and talked to him for a brief period of time. Then, grabbing his black satchel from the rear floor of his car, he methodically climbed the wooden steps of the side porch.

"Good morning, Mrs. Stevenson," he would say at the screen door. And the next thing you knew he was thumping Glen's chest and Glen was saying "ah," once again.

At the side door it was always the same look he gave to Mom-a look that seemed to say, "I'm sorry, Mrs. Stevenson. There's nothing more I can do."

Just as faithful, on Saturdays, was Mrs. Pangborn. Mrs. Pangborn was a reverent lady, in her early forties, who came to love Glen so. Single-handedly, she had started a Bible school up the road, at Five Points, and now she was fighting to 'claim this family for the Lord.' Her long, straight hair was tied tightly to her scalp and rolled neatly in a high bun that sat on top of her head. She wore no lipstick, rouge, or perfume, claiming if God had wanted her to have rosy cheeks and red lips, He would have made her so. Dad could have debated this, and would have, as he had so often at other times, but now he was so thankful that Mrs. Pangborn took such a liking to Glen that he dared not discourage her.

And so it was that each Saturday morning Mrs. Pangborn sat near Glen's bed reading proper verses from the Good Book, comforting his soul, and praying that God would lay His loving and healing hands upon this weak and sickened body.

Each day Aunt Rose and Uncle Clyde 'popped in' to help take care of the brood of heathens so Mom could spend more time with Glen.

"There's no time for monkey business!" Aunt Rose snapped time and time again at each of us. Each time she was pulling Henry or one of us disrespectful children by the ear, and leading us to our chores. Aunt Rose was rough with us and claimed there was no place in this world, or the next, for any child who was lazy and disrespectful. Each of us had our chores to do and "by hook or crook we were going to do them!"

Hanging the clothes out to dry, one hot day, Aunt Rose stripped to her bra and threw her blouse to the ground. It was Eddie who noticed her first and soon our snickers filled the air of the backyard.

"If you boys can have the luxury of stripping bare to your waists anytime you feel like it, then by freckles on a bat we girls can strip to our

bras!" Aunt Rose shouted over the clothesline. *"And there will be no further talk on the subject!"*

That's when Aunt Rose twisted my ear. "You're too good, kid. Sometimes ya gotta be bad to be good. Good Lord, someday you're liable to grow up and become one of those preacher men. Heaven forbid! Trouble is, you're about as good as Henry is bad. He needs a little more good in him and you need a little more bad in you. Good golly! Where did I go wrong in raisin' this brood of hea- thens?" Then she shook her head in disgust and walked away. Dad stood and watched her walk away. Then slapping his knee I heard him laugh harder than ever before.

In the evening, when we had retired to the house, there was law and order. Night after night we were to be on our best behavior. There would be no fighting, no arguing, and no unnecessary noises. Aunt Rose demanded respect and she received it. She was not a churchgoer, as Dad referred to regular church attendees, but Aunt Rose believed in God. There was a purpose for her life, "Even if it's simply helpin' Lydia raise this 'brood of brats!" she often teased.

Even with Mom having more time to spend with Glen, there was little or no improvement in his health. Night after night there were the same sounds coming up the stairs and Mom was con- cerned with Glen's coloring. "He's so pale and so weak!" She wept one day in Aunt Rose's arms.

One evening, I took my lucky stone from my sock drawer and stood at the threshold of Esther's and Roberta's bedroom. "Esther!" I whispered. "I want t' tell ya somethin'. Can I come in?"

Esther pulled the covers firmly around her neck. "Sure," she said, "come on in."

I scooted across the wood floor and quietly curled at the foot of Esther's and Roberta's bed. "I heard Dad tellin' Mom that this house is a jinx and that's why Glen's sick, Esther. He even said we were gonna move as soon as we could." I paused as though I wanted to cry. "I don't want t' move from this house, Esther. I like livin' here on Anglin' Road." I wanted to tell her more. I wanted to tell her about that man we met at the bridge. I wanted to tell her that I was madder than a wet hornet because Henry said that horrible man wanted to take Glen from us and split our family up. But I didn't tell her. I wanted to tell her about my lucky stone. But I couldn't. That was my secret. I clutched it secretly in the palm of my fist. "I love it here on Anglin' Road, Esther."

"And so does everyone else love it here on Anglin' Road," Esther assured me. "Even Dad. He just says stuff like that to get everything off his chest. He doesn't really mean it. Believe me; Dad loves Anglin' Road as much as we do."

"As much as I love Anglin' Road I'd leave, too, if I thought it would make Glen better," I said.

"Believe me, Carl, it's not Anglin' Road. Glen's just sick, and it doesn't matter where we live. That's the way muscular dystrophy is."

I stared through the night air, searching now for the truth in Esther's eyes. "Ya know what, Esther?" I whispered bashfully. "I did somethin' t' night, but I don't want the others t' know 'bout it."

"What's that?" Esther whispered back.

"I prayed, Esther. I did jist like I heard Mrs. Pangborn tell Glen ya must do. I prayed real hard. An' I asked God t' forgive me for all the bad thin's I ever did."

Esther reached down and held my small hand in hers. "That's really good, Carl. I'm really proud of you. That's what Roberta and I do every night before we go to bed. That's what you're supposed to do."

"I prayed for Glen, Esther. Mrs. Pangborn said God would hear our prayers if we 'fessed our sins first. I wanted God t' hear this prayer, Esther. An' ya know what?"

"What?" Esther whispered.

"I think He heard me. I think Glen's gonna be all right now."

"You know what?" Esther whispered again as she rubbed my head.

"What?"

"I think you're right, because God does answer prayers. With you, Roberta, Mom, and me praying, we can't go wrong!"

"Do ya think Mom prays, Esther? I never heard her."

"That's because she's not the boastful type. She prays when she's alone, though. I can tell by the look in her eyes. You can always tell by their eyes. Besides, nobody could go through life with her outlook and not be a prayerful person. In fact, I wouldn't be surprised if Dad and the other boys pray, too. In fact, I'll bet even Aunt Rose does!"

"Aunt Rose? Do ya really think so, Esther?"

"Sure! They're all the same. They just like to play tough, that's all."

I crawled quietly from the bed. "I guess I'll go t' bed now, Esther. Thanks for listenin'."

"You betcha. Now, you get some sleep, and remember, Carl, God does answer prayers. Goodnight."

"Imagine that," I whispered to myself as I quietly shuffled my feet across the floor, "even Aunt Rose prays!"

22 | 'Pillow Talk'

Sickness was certainly nothing new to our household. In the early spring the cold March rains had filled the air with viruses that brought sore throats to nearly all of us and at least two of us were bedridden at a time with high fevers and delirium. Once one of us had passed the crises another took our place in bed. Mom had always said that I took it worse than any of the others. Once, in the past winter, I was so sick with a sore throat I could hardly swallow. Mom put two sofa chairs face to face, as a makeshift bed, and watched me throughout the long, cold nights trying to keep my fever down. On my worst night, my fever zoomed to 105 degrees, and Mom, dampening my forehead with a cool, wet cloth became alarmed as I rose from my makeshift bed, screaming because in my delirium I could see someone dragging Mom across the ceiling by her hair.

But this had all passed and soon I was running around the house as though I had never been sick. But with Glen it was different. Muscular dystrophy was taking its toll on his already weak body.

One Sunday morning Aunt Rose and Uncle Clyde came to our house earlier than usual. There was a peculiar twinkle in their eyes. Aunt Rose summoned Dad and told him to "Hook up the radio."

"It's nearly eight o'clock, Aunt Rose," Glen reminded her, "and you know I always listen to 'Pillow Talk'."

I know that!" Aunt Rose snapped. "What do you take me for – a dummy? I just want to make sure I don't miss it!"

Aunt Rose proceeded to turn the dial until she came upon WPIC from Sharon, Pennsylvania. Upon finding the correct station, she set the volume just right, set herself down in the chair beside Glen's bed and winked to Mom.

Nobody knew what Aunt Rose and Uncle Clyde were up to, but both commanded us children to be especially quiet; Uncle Clyde in his special teasing way and Aunt Rose in her stern, bossy way. Uncle Clyde pulled Roberta to his lap and cupped his left ear with his hand so he would not miss a word the announcer was about to say.

Soon the theme song for 'Pillow Talk' came across the air and the gentleman with the mellow voice began with his usual greetings to one and all. "His name is Larry Vincent," Glen reminded everyone. Aunt Rose wriggled in her seat and held a finger to her lips. All must be especially quiet now.

Glen's eyes glowed suspiciously now, but still he was uncertain what would happen next. Everyone became anxious. Mom and Dad looked to each other for answers, but neither had any idea what Uncle Clyde and Aunt Rose had up their sleeves. Larry Vincent spoke of a shut-in from Farrell, Pennsylvania and then played a song.

After the song was over Aunt Rose put her fingers to her lips and whispered that we should all be extra quiet. "We are told that Glen Lovegood, of Hartford, Ohio, considers 'Pillow Talk' his favorite program and faithfully listens each Sunday morning," Larry said. "Glen has muscular dystrophy and we understand that he has been ill and confined to bed for some time now. We are also told his greatest thrill is to listen to the numerous requests we play for others each Sunday morning.

"Well, Glen, we just want you to know that each of us here, at WPIC, is constantly thinking of you and you are in our every prayer. We understand that you're quite a singer, Glen, and that one of your favorite songs is 'Whispering Hope.' Well, Glen, we're going to spin that record for you right now and hope that it cheers your day just a little. God bless you, and get well real soon!"

In a moment the beautiful words of "Whispering Hope" filled the air while around Glen's bed happy eyes twinkled with excitement. Glen looked to Mom and then to Aunt Rose and Uncle Clyde. Aunt Rose smiled to Glen and patted his hand. Mom squeezed his other hand and tears of joy welled up inside her eyes.

"Gee!" Uncle Clyde laughed aloud when the song was over. "I didn't know I was in the presence of a celebrity!" Then, grasping Glen's hand firmly, he shook it vigorously. "Good grief," he laughed louder, "could I have your autograph?"

"You seem to know just what to do to pick a person's soul up when it's down so low, Rose," Mom said. She spoke now as the two entered the kitchen. "There never were any truer friends than you and Clyde."

Mom wanted to say more, but Aunt Rose interrupted her. "Now, what in the blazes are you talkin' about? Oh, you think - now - wait a minute! Don't go thinking that Clyde and I had anything to do with this, Lydia! All I know is, Clyde and I came out here to get the brood in order before company sets in and we don't know anything else."

Mom wrapped her apron around her waist and tied it behind her back. Handing another apron to Aunt Rose, she smiled and brushed the tears from her eyes. "Then I suggest we get the potatoes peeled and cooked before the brood starves to death," she said.

23 | Medicine From Uncle Slim

Soon after dinner was over, Uncle Slim and Grandma pulled up our long driveway. Uncle Slim tooted his horn, turned his car around by the barn, and parked near the side porch. He hopped out of his car, gave that look that said he was pretending he had been drinking more of 'the hard stuff' and wobbled to Grandma's side of the car. He laughed that silly 'drunk' laugh and then helped Grandma to the side porch. He wobbled back to the car, reached to the rear seat, and pulled out a long whip. Waving it high above his head, he snapped it back and forth until you could hear the cracks echoing across the sky.

"Where's the cattle?" he called in his drunken voice. Then he snapped the whip high above his head once more. "There they are!" he shouted when he spotted Eddie, Wesley, and me standing in the back yard. "Whoopy!" he yelled as he ran toward us with wobbly legs and his whip snapping high above his head. "Hee, hee, hee!" he laughed as he snapped the whip, rapping it around Eddie's ankle. Eddie kicked the whip loose from his ankle and we began running to get away from Uncle Slim.

"You can't get away from me!" He laughed louder as the whip snapped above his head. "I've lassoed tougher cattle than you, before!"

"Land sakes alive!" Grandma cried from the kitchen window. *"That fool's gonna hurt one of those kids with that thing! I swear he's a bigger kid than all the rest put together!"* She made a move to the

kitchen door to shout out to Uncle Slim that he must settle down for Glen's sake, as well as ours, but it was too late. Before she got to the door, Uncle Slim had rounded up Eddie, Wesley, and me, chasing madly after us as a cowboy chases after a loose calf.

Crack! Snap! The whip echoed loudly as Uncle Slim whisked it high above his head in hot pursuit after us. Past the outhouse we ran, circling the house three times like wild Indians around a ring of wagons. *"Help! Help!"* we screamed for our lives. Uncle Slim snapped the whip louder, enjoying every minute of his imaginary rodeo.

From his bedroom window, Glen watched the exhibition as first Eddie, Wesley, and I zipped past the window screaming with floods of tears streaming down our faces. Then, just as quickly, Uncle Slim ran past Glen's window snapping his whip and laughing till he almost fell to the ground.

No sooner had Uncle Slim flashed past Glen's window when Glen and Mom spotted Aunt Rose zipping past the window in hot pursuit of Uncle Slim, waving her fist high in the air. Her face was red with anger and fatigue. When Glen saw Aunt Rose chasing Uncle Slim past his window he began to laugh for the first time in weeks. Mom was so happy to see Glen laugh that she almost laughed too, in spite of her concern for our safety.

Finally, Uncle Slim became exhausted and stopping by the car he doubled over with laughter, slapping his knees, calling funny remarks to us as we ran frantically into the house. In a few moments, Aunt Rose met Uncle Slim at the car and from the windows of the house everyone could see that some heated words were being said. Quickly, the laughter disappeared from Uncle Slim's face as Aunt Rose continued to wave her arms in anger.

After a few minutes, Aunt Rose came into the house and Uncle Slim put his whip back into his car. No one knew exactly what Aunt Rose had said to Uncle Slim, but for the remainder of the day Uncle Slim would not come into the house. He just sat upon the hood of his car and pouted like a baby.

When Glen heard that Uncle Slim would not come into the house it made him laugh all the harder. From his bedroom window, he could see Uncle Slim perched upon the hood of his car, barely moving for what seemed hours. For the first time in weeks Glen had had a good laugh and Grandma swore there was more color in his cheeks than the week before.

24 | Showers of Blessings

Wednesday morning, Roberta jumped off the side porch and rushed down the driveway to the mailbox at Anglin' Road. Soon she was running back up the hill with excitement sparkling in her eyes. In her hands were stacks of cards and letters. "Just look at these!" she shouted as she approached Mom at the side porch. A wide smile spread across her pretty face. "These are cards! They're all addressed to Glen! They're from everywhere! Just look at this," she continued excitedly, handing individual cards to Mom. "Here's one from West Middlesex - another from Sharon - and here's one from Brookfield. There must be forty cards here!"

Mom wiped her hands on her side and spread her apron out so Roberta could let the cards fall in. Sunshine seemed to spread across Mom's face. Once again a ray of hope glimmered in her eyes. "Showers of blessings!" She smiled as the cards dropped to the apron below. Sifting the cards with her tiny fingers, Mom lifted her eyes toward the sky above. "Pure and simple showers of blessings!"

As she entered the house we all trailed Mom to Glen's bedroom. "Look here, young man," Mom said. She let the cards fall to Glen's bed. "It seems to me we do have a celebrity among us. The last time I saw this many cards was at Christmas time - and they didn't all come at once."

Glen looked at the cards and then to Mom. His eyes shone brightly now. "It must be because of '*Pillow Talk*'," he said.

Robert grabbed the handle at the foot of Glen's bed and cranked it to an upright position. Roberta propped a pillow behind his head.

One by one, Mom opened the cards and handed each to Glen as we all gathered around his bed. "Here's one from another boy with muscular dystrophy," Glen said. "He's about my age and wants me t' write back."

"I think that would be great, Glen," Esther exclaimed. "You probably have a lot in common."

"I wonder if he's a celebrity like you," Robert teased.

Glen set the card aside and Mom handed him another. "There are a lot of good people in the world, Mom. Just look at these!" Glen pointed to the cards being passed around the room. "It makes me feel real good, Mom, just to know people care. It makes me want t' help others when I get better, Mom!"

"When I get better!" Glen's words repeated themselves over and over again in my mind. It was the first time since Glen's illness we had heard him refer to "getting over" his illness.

That evening Mom slipped quietly into her bedroom and closed the door. At the bottom of the stairwell we could hear her soft cries through her bedroom door. "Maybe you should go in and see what's wrong with Mom," I said to Esther and Roberta.

"Just let her cry," Roberta suggested as she guided me out the front door and to the front porch. "That's right," Esther agreed. "Mom's been through an awful lot lately. Besides, they're only tears of joy anyhow. She's just thankful for all the nice people sending all those cards to Glen."

"She needs to cry it all out of her system," Roberta agreed. "It's just like when Dad screamed and hollered at Mom and all of us when he was out of work so long. He was just getting it out of his system. Mom's doing the same thing. She's just doing it in a different way."

I stepped off the front porch and shook my head in disbelief. How crying could make someone happier was beyond my understanding. However, if Esther and Roberta said it would, then I would ponder the thought.

Somewhere in the tall maple trees that shaded the front lawn a woodpecker hammered loudly. I looked up. A late summer breeze brushed gently against my tanned face and carried with it the sweet smell of wild roses. I took a deep breath. "The sweetest aroma this side of heaven! It's the aroma that always accompanies angels when they appear," I remembered Mom saying one day. Could it be that Glen's guardian angel was riding in with the same aroma I now smelled? I believed it was.

25 | A Terrible Thing Happens to Betty Jane

"Mom, Roberta and I want to go to church," Esther announced at the kitchen sink.

Mom turned around, quite surprised. "Why on earth did you say that?"

"Because we've both been thinking about it for a long time, Mom. There's a new minister at the Methodist church. We heard he's really good. And we decided we want to go," Roberta said.

Mom dipped her hands into the sink and scrubbed another dish. "You know your dad won't have anything to do with churches. He says there's not an honest preacher among the whole lot of them."

"Well, Dad doesn't have to go, Mom. We're only asking to let us go," Esther returned.

"Well, how on earth would you get there? You know your dad isn't going to drive you there."

Esther wiped her hands on her apron and smiled to Mom. "We'll walk, Mom."

"Walk? For heaven's sake! That's two or three miles to the center of Hartford. I can't let you walk to church. Who knows what could happen to you on those wooded roads, especially with that Bert Becker running loose. "

"But Mom! That's not fair to Bert Becker. He's never hurt anyone."

"Well, just the same," Mom said, "I don't want you walking those roads alone."

"What if Henry and Robert walked us to church, Mom? They don't have to go to church. All we're asking is that they walk us to church."

Mom swirled around and broke into a smile. "You know that would please me to no end. You know your Aunt Gloria would be so proud of you. She's been with the Salvation Army for so many years now I forgot. Every time she writes she asks if you two girls are in church yet. You just go and ask your brothers if they're willing to help us. If they agree, we'll mention it to your dad at supper tonight. I don't want to keep any secrets from him. I see no reason why he would object."

At the supper table Dad looked down at Esther and Roberta and said, "Of course I don't object t' your goin' t' church. I think that would be nice. And Henry and Robert will walk you t' church. All I ask is that you don't expect me t' take you." He turned to face Mom and then continued. "Lord knows I've had my fill of preachers in my time. You kids don't know it, but I know that Bible inside an' out. Oh, don't look so surprised. At the Home us boys went t' church every Sunday. We were forced t' go. They shoved it down our throats. Well, maybe I shouldn't say it that way. I'm not much for talkin' about it, but I believe in it. It's just those dog-gone preachers that turn me off. They're always askin' for money, but never really carin' about the poor people. Seems they only care about people with money." He took a bite of food, and then continued. "Now look at that! You got my dandruff up over those confounded preacher folk. I will tell you this. If I ever find a preacher man that feels like I do I'll recognize him in a heartbeat. Then maybe I'll even go t' church." He looked to me and winked. "Don't think I'll have t' worry about that for a long while."

Next Sunday morning Henry and Robert walked Esther and Roberta to the Methodist church in Hartford. It was then Henry and Robert saw the stranger who had asked all the questions the day we were fishing at the bridge.

"Jist like Dad said," Henry told me later, "he was dressed t' kill. He was just leavin' from Sunday school. I guess he wasn't stayin' for church. But he strutted outta church like he was some kinda big shot king."

"Did he recognize you and Robert?"

"Naw. His nose was too high in the air! But if he ever says anythin' again, I'll tell him where t' get off! Nobody's gonna tell me we're not as good as somebody else jist because we're not rich!"

My blood was boiling for the first time in a long time. "I don't understand it, Henry. Why does he care about us? What difference does it make t' him if we're rich or poor?"

Henry sat down on the front porch. Then, looking up to me he said, "Well, believe it or not, Carl, some people don't have nothin' else t' do with their lives. He must think God called him t' save us from this terrible life we live here on Anglin' Road."

"Terrible life?" I shouted. "We don't have a terrible life. We have a great life! I like livin' here on Anglin' Road. We have more fun than anyone I know and I don't care if other people think we're poor. We're not."

"Well, I've heard of people jist like him before. They ain't happy 'til they split families up. That's why he was askin' 'bout Glen. I told Uncle Clyde 'bout him and Uncle Clyde said he's an evil man. He said he's prob'ly one of those people who thinks all handicapped people, like Glen, should be livin' in some home where nurses are 'round all day t' take care of him."

"But Glen's happy here. And he's our brother. They don't have no right t' take him or any one of us away." I was getting angrier by the minute.

"Come on, pal, enough of this talk. Let's get Robert an' Eddie an' go fishin.' "

We weren't fishing long when Robert got bored. He set his pole down on the bank and began to wander through the trees behind him.

"Where are ya goin'?" I asked.

"I'm bored," he said. "I'm goin' for a walk through the woods. Do ya want t' come with me?"

"Sure!" I said as I set my pole to the ground.

"I want t' see what Lovers' Lane looks like," he whispered to me. "I heard it's really beautiful this time of year."

"But Mom told us to stay away from there," I reminded Robert.

"I know, but we'll only peek at it t' see what it looks like."

We were too far into the woods for me to turn back now. Anyhow, I wanted to see Lovers' Lane, too.

As Robert and I neared Lovers' Lane we could hear some screaming and rustling as though someone was fighting. Then there was the whinnying of a horse. Suddenly, a short man with straggly white hair and a long white beard darted out of the woods, running rapidly from Lovers' Lane.

"It's Bert Becker!" Robert shouted.

Bert Becker took a quick look at Robert and me. His face was scratched badly and blood streamed down his cheeks. A look of fear and hopelessness penetrated his deep, blue eyes. Quickly, he turned and then he ran deeper into the woods. In the distance, across the large cathedral, Robert and I heard a man's deep voice calling anxiously. We rushed up a small ridge to a clearing where all the trees were removed and splendid, beautiful, blue-green grass lay on the ground as though it were a beautiful, green carpet. Tall trees surrounded this large, grassy opening; its branches reaching out to each other. Sunlight burst through the golden leaves above, raining down showers of light that glistened like sparkling chandeliers. It was the most beautiful sight I had ever seen.

On the far side of the cathedral, Betty Jane lay unconscious on the green grass. Blood ran down her pale face. Through the towering trees, in the direction of Anglin' Road, Robert and I heard a car's engine rev up and then speed quickly down Anglin' Road toward the bridge, where Henry and Eddie were fishing.

Across the cathedral, a tall, thin man and a young boy about Robert's age came hurrying around a long lane that came from the direction of another road. Robert and I rushed to Betty Jane's side. "What in the world is going on here?" the tall man shouted as he approached Betty Jane. It was the man Robert and I heard calling through the woods. "What has happened to this young girl," he asked, panting and nearly out of breath. He bent down and lifted Betty Jane's small, limp hand. "Why this young girl is unconscious and hurting badly." Then, looking to Robert and me, he said, "What do you two know about this? What happened here?"

"We don't know," Robert said. "We were walkin' through the woods when we heard Betty Jane screamin'. Then we saw Bert Becker runnin' away from Betty Jane."

"Then you know this girl?" he asked.

"Yes, she's our neighbor."

"Did you say Bert Becker?" he asked with a puzzled look upon his face.

"Yes, we saw him runnin' through the woods. We didn't see him hurt Betty Jane," Robert said.

"Why in all my years I never heard of Bert Becker doing anything like this before. We don't live here. We only hunt here. But I've heard of Bert Becker and this doesn't sound like something he would do." The man looked again to Betty Jane. "We'd better get her to the hospital immediately," he said as he scooped Betty Jane into his strong arms. "We're parked just down the road a piece. We heard this young girl screaming and hurried down here." As he hurried down the long lane with Betty Jane in his arms we heard him say, "I just knew something like this would happen in here some day!"

Robert and I took Jesse by her reigns and led her down the long lane to Bushnell Campbell Road and then to Anglin' Road and finally toward home. Henry stood at the bridge with his fishing pole in his hand. "What are ya doin' with Jesse?" he asked with a surprised look. "Where's Betty Jane?"

"She's on her way t' the hospital," I said.

"Hospital? Why in the world is she goin' t' the hospital?"

"Jist sit down and we'll tell ya all 'bout it," Robert said.

Eddie joined us at the bridge and he and Henry listened quietly while Robert and I told what had happened at Lovers' Lane.

"Then I'll bet that man who sped by here awhile ago had somethin' t' do with this," Henry spoke when we finished telling our story. "I was standin' on the bridge when this man, in an old Chevy, went speedin' by here. I was afraid he was goin' t' hit me the way he was speedin'. I didn't get a good look at him though. But there was somethin' 'bout that car. It looked very familiar. But maybe I jist saw one like it in the magazine. I jist can't place it." Henry shook his head as though he were ashamed that he couldn't remember just where he had seen that car. "I sure hope he did it and not Bert Becker." Then he took Jesse from Robert and said, "Let's take Jesse home an' let Dad explain everythin' to Betty Jane's parents."

<hr>

"You were right in tellin' that man who took Betty Jane t' the hospital that you saw Bert Becker runnin' from Lovers' Lane, boys," Dad said. "But I hope you're right. I hope it wasn't Bert Becker. I'm hopin' it was the man you saw at the bridge, Henry."

"He went by fast! But there was jist somethin' 'bout that car."

"Well, I'm not as convinced as you and the boys are that it wasn't Bert Becker," Mom said. "Why on earth was his face all scratched up and blood on his cheeks? And why was he running away if he didn't do it? Seems to me he would have stayed there and tried to help that poor girl if he's as innocent as you all say he is." Mom turned and walked up the steps to the back porch. "That poor, poor girl," she said softly.

"Well, you boys go get your supper an' I'll take care of every-thin'," Dad said as he took Jesse by her reins and headed down Anglin' Road to Betty Jane's house.

Later that day, Constable Snyder came to our house and questioned Robert and me.

"We saw Bert Becker runnin' from Lovers' Lane with scratches on his face an' blood runnin' down his cheek," Robert told him. "But we don't think he did this horrible thing t' Betty Jane. He jist couldn't."

"If he didn't do it, then who did?"

"Maybe it was the man who sped by me when I was on the bridge," Henry said.

"Well, I suppose anything is possible. But just because a man drives down a road at top speed doesn't mean he committed a crime. There's more evidence pointing to Bert Becker. And that's why we need to take him in for questioning," Constable Snyder said. "I need to know just why he was running from the scene of the crime." He took his hat from his head and scratched above his left ear. "I just can't believe Bert Becker would be involved in anything like this. Still, what was he running from? And why was his face scratched so badly with blood running down his cheeks? It sounds to me like Betty Jane must have scratched him badly when he pulled her off her horse." He placed his hat back on his head and tipped it forward. "Oh, gosh. I don't know what to think. I still can't believe he did that horrible thing to that poor girl." Then he stepped down from the side porch and headed toward his car. "Well, I'll get a few volunteers and we'll go into the woods and get him. It's something I don't like to do, but I have to."

Later that day Constable Snyder and a few men from Hartford picked up Bert Becker and held him in a nearby jail until a trial would be held. On his way home Constable Snyder stopped at our house to explain what had happened. With his foot propped on the running board of his car he twisted his hat and slapped it on his knee. "He never said a word in his own defense. He never told us why he was there, what he saw, why he was running away or why his face was scratched and bleeding." Constable Snyder said directly to Dad and Mom. "But I told him what you two boys said about believing he had nothing to do with all this," he said, turning to look at Robert and me. "And I told him how your whole family was praying for him. And I'll tell you the God's truth, boys, I saw such a pleasant look on his face." He turned to face Dad and Mom. "Actually, I would say it was a look of peace that I can't explain. I think it meant so much for him to know you people really care for him." Once again, he slapped his knee with his hat and jumped into his car without saying another word. In a moment he was speeding up Anglin' Road and out of sight.

"You never know when a man like Bert Becker just might escape from that tiny jail and hide in those woods again," Grandma said. "You girls be extra careful."

"Maybe Betty Jane will come out of that coma real soon, Grandma, and prove that it wasn't Bert Becker who hurt her. Maybe she'll be able to identify the man who really did it to her," Esther said.

"Perhaps she will, Esther. I pray you're right. Until then, you just mind your p's and q's and be very careful. It's bad enough that your brother lays in his sick bed, sick as can be. Your mother sure doesn't need you two girls hurt, too."

Mom took one quick look at Esther and then Roberta, as though to say she agreed with Grandma. Then, as she walked to the kitchen sink she spoke to everyone in the kitchen. "I assure you the truth will come out someday and whoever did this to Betty Jane, whether it was Bert Becker or someone else, will some day pay for hurting Betty Jane as he did."

26 | "It's Larry Vincent From 'Pillow Talk!'"

Each day there were more cards and each of us fought over who would get the mail the next day. Some days there were only four or five cards, but following each new *'Pillow Talk'* program there were always more. Mom displayed the cards throughout Glen's bedroom and finally, each Saturday evening she gathered them up and neatly arranged them in a large album that Glen could keep for years to come.

Day after day, Glen received his new cards and gratefully he looked through his album. He wondered about the people who sent these marvelous cards and wished he could thank each one for the joy his or her card had brought. Though he weighed no more than eighty pounds and every rib and bone protruded through his skin he was becoming healthier and stronger with each new day. His color had come back to near normal and he asked to sit in his wheelchair. He talked of this year's musical show coming soon, and how he, Esther, and Roberta would need to practice.

One Sunday afternoon, while Grandma, Uncle Slim, Aunt Rose and Uncle Clyde were at the house a green car pulled up the driveway. On the side of the car were the letters "WPIC".

"For Pete's sake!" Aunt Rose bellowed. *"It must be Larry Vincent, from 'Pillow Talk'!"*

The young man parked his car in the driveway, walked to the side door, and introduced himself and his wife.

"Come right in," Dad said as he greeted them with a warm handshake. "This sure is some surprise!" Dad then introduced Larry to each of the adults and then pointed to us children. "This is the 'brood', as we call them 'round here." He laughed and rubbed my head.

Larry Vincent appeared to be a humble man and yet there was an air of dignity surrounding him that held us children spellbound. He was tall, a handsome man. His hair was styled like Errol Flynn's and he gave the appearance of a movie star, himself. His wife, Alice, too, was beautiful. Her long auburn hair hung to her shoulders and her green eyes sparkled like millions of tiny stars. As she entered the side door, the entire room filled with sweet, lilac perfume.

Dad led them to Glen who was now seated in his wheelchair beside his bed. And there, though they had known each other for some time, the two met for the first time.

"This is indeed an honor," Larry said as he extended his hand to Glen.

Though his elbows were permanently bent from muscular dystrophy, and Glen would never fully extend his arms again, he lifted his feeble hand to Larry and greeted him with a warm handshake. "Thank you, Mr. Vincent. The pleasure is indeed mine." Glen blushed as he spoke. "I never dreamed you would come t' visit me."

"The truth is, I don't make it a habit to visit people we dedicate our songs and time to. Somehow, I found myself wanting to meet you. I'd like to get to know more about you, Glen." His voice was mellow; each word was annunciated precisely as he did on radio. "I know you're quite a singer, but I understand you play a ukulele, too." He looked again to Glen's frail body and though he said nothing, his eyes told how his heart was aching for Glen.

"Yes, but I do owe much of that talent to my Uncle Slim, though." Glen blushed again.

Uncle Slim stood at the door to Glen's room. He puffed his chest and nodded to Larry.

"And I hear you're also an artist! Is there anything you can't do?" Larry smiled and touched Glen's scrawny arm.

"There are some of his drawin's hangin' on the wall," Dad spoke now, as he pointed to several pictures hanging throughout the room. "As ya can see he enjoys paintin' landscape scenes."

Mom pulled the paintings from the wall and handed each to Larry Vincent.

"Amazing!" Larry laughed proudly as he studied each painting carefully.

"How rude of us," Aunt Rose interrupted. "We haven't even offered you two a seat, yet. Please do have a seat, both of you." She motioned to two chairs beside Glen's bed.

"Of course," Dad said. "How rude of me! Please do have a seat!"

"And what about me?" Larry laughed. "I haven't even introduced my better half to you, Glen." He turned and apologized to his wife. Putting his arm around her shoulder, he pulled her close. "This is my lovely wife, Alice. And please do call us Larry and Alice rather than Mr. and Mrs. Vincent. Mr. and Mrs. make us feel old." He laughed again.

Taking the seat closer to Glen, Larry said, "I'd like everybody to listen to the good news that came into our newsroom just before I left. Please listen carefully." He looked around the room and began to smile. Not a word was said as we waited anxiously to hear the good news. "Are you ready?" He smiled. "Betty Jane came out of her coma today!"

"Oh! Thank God!" Grandma said and then pulled her small hanky from her apron pocket and wiped her tears.

"Thank you, Lord! Thank you!" Mom cried.

"Prayers do come true!' Glen said softly.

Aunt Rose pulled Esther and Roberta close to her side and then hugged them tightly.

"She said she doesn't remember the man who attacked her," Larry spoke on. "But she does think she has seen him. I guess she hasn't been in town long enough to know too many people, but she thinks she has seen the man. She thinks she may have seen him right here on Anglin' Road. She claims there has been an older man looking very funny at her when he would pass her somewhere around the bridge. She thinks if she ever sees the man again, or even a picture of him, she'll be able to identify him. But there is one thing she does know. She's positive it wasn't Bert Becker!"

"*Halleluiah!*" Aunt Rose shouted and jumped up from her seat. "I'm so happy for that Bert fellow! Now, how's that young girl doing?"

"She's going to be just fine," Larry said. "She still needs plenty of rest. And no one's allowed to see her until we find the man who did this to her."

"Oh, our prayers have been answered!" Mom said. Then she began to cry again.

Uncle Clyde hugged Robert and me. "Your worries are finally over, boys," he said.

"And Betty Jane is gonna be fine, now," I said.

"Yes, and Betty Jane is going to be fine! *Halleluiah! Halleluiah!*" Esther shouted.

"I'm just honored that I could bring you folks that good news. You see, the person who told me about you, Glen, also told me about Betty Jane. So I knew there was a connection between the two of you," Larry said.

"And what 'bout Bert Becker? Is he out of jail yet?" Dad asked.

"Yes, he is, I'm excited to tell you. He was being released as I was on my way here."

"Hallelujah! Hallelujah! Hallelujah!" Aunt Rose said softly, as a prayer.

"The interesting thing is," Larry Vincent spoke again, "according to Betty Jane, the last thing she remembers is the other man pulling her off her horse. In that split second she remembers seeing Bert Becker tackling him. She claims Bert Becker came out of nowhere to help her and started wrestling with this man. Then she fell and remembers no more. According to Betty Jane, when Bert Becker jumped that man, whoever he was, he took a branch of a tree lying beside him and kept hitting Bert Becker in the face with it."

"That explains the scratches on his face an' the blood Carl an' I saw runnin' down his face," Robert explained.

"And that explains why he was runnin' away when that other man an' his son came down the lane yellin'," I said. "He thought they would think he was hurtin' Betty Jane because the man who actually did hurt Betty Jane was runnin' away from the scene. The man who was hurtin' Betty Jane decided t' run t' his car when he heard the other man an' his son yellin'. Wow! It all makes sense now!"

"Sure," Robert said. "I'll bet Bert Becker was knocked unconscious, too, an' woke up t' see that man he wrestled with runnin' through the woods. When he heard the other man an' his son comin' he knew he had t' get away in a hurry or be blamed, as he was. He didn't know we would see him in the woods."

"My goodness!" Uncle Clyde laughed. "These two aren't only heroes; they're also a couple of fine detectives!"

Robert shook his head in disbelief. "Perhaps we're good detectives," he said, "but the real hero is Bert Becker."

"Well, I must admit I'm a little ashamed of myself for thinking it might have been Bert Becker," Mom said. "But I'm so happy now that it wasn't. Here I was thinking such bad thoughts about Bert

Becker and in the end he was really a true to the bone hero." Mom wiped a tear from her eye. "My, oh, my! I guess I had a closed mind, didn't I? Nevertheless, our prayers have been answered for Betty Jane. Praise the Lord she's out of her coma and feeling just fine."

"Well, you're certainly not the only one thankful that that poor girl's doin' fine now. And you're not the only one who should apologize to that Bert fellow. I'm just as ashamed as you are, Lydia," Grandma said. "I just pray they'll bring that cruel man to justice, soon."

"Well, I don't think either of you need t' be ashamed of anythin'," Dad said. "I know I told the boys I didn't think Bert Becker did it, but t' tell you the truth I wasn't so sure myself. I'm just so doggone glad he didn't." Then he turned and winked at Robert and me.

Larry smiled. "I'm so happy I was able to bring you folks the good news." Looking to Glen he said, "Perhaps you and your family would like to hear some stories from people I've met while doing 'Pillow Talk'."

I brushed the tears from my eyes as Larry began telling stories of people from *Pillow Talk*" and exciting tales of his adventures on radio. My mind kept going from Betty Jane to Bert Becker and back to Larry Vincent. What a day this had been. First, Larry Vincent had come to our house. Then Larry had told us of the exciting news of Betty Jane. I looked at Robert and he, too, was rubbing tears from his eyes. He looked to me and we both smiled as Larry continued his tales of *Pillow Talk*.

"These are his most valued treasures," Mom said when Larry finished speaking. In her hands, she held the album of Glen's cards. "He'll treasure these forever, thanks to you and 'Pillow Talk'."

Larry and Alice leafed through the pages of cards, stopping occasionally to read some of the personal notes. Alice's eyes began to moisten. "These cards are worth more than gold," she said.

"You will stay for supper," Mom interrupted as she took the album from Alice. "The table is set."

"My goodness!" Larry said with a startled look. "I can't believe it's that late already! Time does fly when you're with wonderful people." He stole a glance to Alice and then back to Mom. "Is it possible to ask one favor before we commit ourselves?" he asked. "I mean Alice and I would truly be blessed if Glen is up to singing one song for us before we leave."

Glen smiled and nodded to Mom. "It's been a long time since I've sung," he said, "but I think it's about time I tried my voice out. If you'll stay for supper Esther, Roberta, and I promise to sing for you."

"It's a deal!" Larry smiled and shook Glen's hand once more.

After supper Alice insisted she help with the dishes. "Most certainly not!" Aunt Rose said while she summoned Esther and Roberta to come quickly to the sink. "You're our guests and no guests are gonna do the dishes in our house!"

Mom chuckled at the fact that Aunt Rose referred to the house as "our house." But then, Aunt Rose and Uncle Clyde were as much a part of the house and home as anyone else. Mom agreed. Alice must not do the dishes.

When the dishes were done the house grew dim as the autumn sun began to set beyond the small orchard. Mom lit the kerosene lamp and set it in the middle of the kitchen table. Grandma lowered her feeble body into an oak, kitchen chair and began fanning her face with a dishtowel. Uncle Clyde stood beside the screen door pulling his pants up with his wrists. Aunt Rose, Mom, and Dad stood at the kitchen sink while Larry and Alice joined Grandma at the table. Around the room we boys positioned ourselves to not interfere with the adults, especially Larry and Alice.

Uncle Slim picked up Glen's ukulele, tuned the strings to his ear's satisfaction, and handed it back to Glen. Soft waves from the kerosene lamp flickered across the ceiling. "We'd like to sing one of our favorite songs," Esther exclaimed as she and Roberta took positions on each side of Glen, "It is No Secret." Then, turning to Roberta, the two hummed the correct key. Glen strummed his ukulele and joined in:

"The chimes of time ring out the news
Another day is through
Someone slipped and fell,
Was that someone you?
You may have longed for added strength,
Your courage to renew,
Do not be discouraged,
For I bring hope to you,
It is no secret—what God can do,
What He's done for others,
He'll do for you,
With arms wide open, He'll pardon you,
It is no secret—what God can do…"

"Beautiful! Just beautiful!" Larry declared as he and Alice rose from their seats, still applauding.

Grandma brushed the tears from her eyes. Mom and Dad beamed proudly while we all smiled approvingly.

"We came here hoping to bring cheer to a young man this afternoon, and here it turns out that my wife and I have been the receivers instead of the givers!" Larry spoke graciously now as he proudly shook Glen's hand. "You've all been so cordial. How can we ever repay you for the joy you've given us today?"

"There's no need t' repay anybody," Dad said as he followed Larry and Alice to the door. "I think we've all been a little blessed t'day. Thank you so much for comin'."

Larry and Alice stood on the side porch and waved through the doorway. "Goodbye everyone! And good luck to you and your sisters in the musical, Glen. We'll be thinking of you. God bless you, now!"

"Thank you!" Glen called in return. "Thank you so much!"

"Imagine that!" we all seemed to chorus as Larry and Alice Vincent drove down the long driveway to Anglin' Road. "Larry Vincent of *'Pillow Talk'* actually came to our house!"

"And Betty Jane is going to be okay," Roberta said.

"And Bert Becker is finally home again," Henry added.

One fact was certain, Grandma had pointed out that evening; Glen was finally over his long illness.

The next morning Mom pushed Glen to the side porch. Teddy scrambled up the wooden steps, propped his front paws upon the arms of Glen's wheelchair and lapped at his face. His tail wagged excitedly. Glen patted Teddy's head. "Did ya miss me, boy?" he asked. And Teddy's tail wagged faster.

27 | Dad's Slipped Disc

At the supper table, Mom buttered Glen a piece of bread and set it near his plate. Taking a quick glance toward the kitchen door she then called out in surprise. "Land Sakes! What in the world is that hanging on our side porch?" Not believing her eyes, she walked to the door and stared through the door window at the porch pillar. "Why… there's something hanging on the pillar of the side porch, Randall," she said. "Good Lord, it looks like a few rabbits hanging from a rope!"

"Rabbits?" Dad questioned as he rose from the kitchen table. "Why in the world would rabbits be hangin' from our side porch?" He walked to the door where Mom stood staring outside and took a quick look. "My goodness!" he said in surprise. "Those aren't rabbits. Those are mink! Three mink, in fact!" He then opened the door and took the mink from the pillar and held them at arm's length while we boys all gathered on the porch beside him.

"Where in the world do you suppose those came from?" Robert asked. "Henry and I didn't put them there."

"I know you didn't," Dad smiled in return. "But I think I know who did."

"Bert Becker!" I shouted out. *"That's who put them there! I just know he did!"*

Dad smiled again as he held the mink so we could all see. "I think you are absolutely correct, Carl. I think Bert Becker snuck up here last night and put them there as a thank you t' all of us."

"A thank you?" Eddie asked. "How are three mink a thank ya?"

"'Cause mink pelts are very expensive. That's why," Henry said.

"I would say so," Dad said. "The last I heard they were runnin' somewhere near thirty dollars apiece. I'd say that's a nice gift. Ninety dollars in all!"

"Ninety dollars!" Esther shouted from inside the screen door. "Do you realize that's nearly enough to pay for four months rent for our house?"

"It sure is, Esther," Dad said as he hung the mink back on the nail. "Can you imagine that? Bert Becker is gonna pay for our next four payments on our rent for this ol' place."

"Oh, my goodness!" Mom declared. "What a kind man he must really be! To think, all this time I had worried so *about* him." She hung her head low as she moved back to the kitchen stove. "Now I worry *for* him," she said. "I guess I learned a good lesson this time. We mustn't judge a book by its cover."

"God bless him!" Dad said, as he took another look at the three mink hanging on the porch pillar. Then he motioned for us all to hurry back to the kitchen table. "I guess we all learned a lesson today."

Mom was now at the kitchen stove pouring more pancake mix into the skillet. "I know this much," she said when all was quiet. "I'm going to pray much harder for Bert Becker and I hope you all do, too. I think he must have a heart as pure as gold." Then turning to place more pancakes on our plates she said, "Why don't you and the boys go fishing at Lake Erie like you've been planning, Randall? Glen's doing so well now." She smiled and patted Glen's hand. "I think Robert and Carl deserve a special treat after what they've been through. Besides, the girls and Glen could use the time away from the boys to practice for the musical."

Dad looked up from his plate with a boyish look in his eyes. Looking to Henry and Robert at the end of the table he said, "Oh, you know I wouldn't mind, Lydia, but I doubt if fishin' in Lake Erie would interest the boys any." Then he smiled to Glen and winked his eye.

"Are you serious?" Robert asked. "That would be like Christmas all over!"

"Are you sure, Lydia?" Dad asked. "You could use the break more than me."

"But I don't like to fish," she teased in return. "Besides, with you and the boys gone it would be like Christmas to the girls and me. Right, girls?"

"Christmas and summer break together!" Roberta laughed.

"I'd say that's a pretty good idea then. All we need t' do is double up on the chores t'day an' we'll head out tomorrow mornin', bright and early."

"But who will milk Daisy Mae while we're gone?" Henry asked. "She'll need to be milked after we'll be gone."

"Oh, my! I hadn't thought of that," Dad said. "That does put a damper on everythin'. We'd better put some thought into this before we go gettin' too excited."

All was quiet for a moment and then Glen spoke with a smile on his face. "I know this sounds silly, but what about Aunt Rose?"

"Aunt Rose?" Dad bellowed. "Why didn't I think of Aunt Rose? Of course! We'll ask Uncle Clyde to go with us an' Aunt Rose can milk Daisy Mae. Now that's a good idea!"

As we all rose from the table to carry our dishes to the sink we all began to chuckle. "I can hear Aunt Rose bossin' ol' Daisy Mae and demandin' more milk or by golly she'll want to know why," I said. Everybody laughed. Then I said, "If I know Aunt Rose, she'll probably twist Daisy Mae's ear like she does ours when we misbehave!"

Uncle Clyde and Aunt Rose arrived before the sun rose the next morning. When Aunt Rose came into the house she snapped Eddie behind the ear. "Are you the one who thinks I can't milk a cow? By golly, when you get home there will be more milk here than you can drink in a week!" Then she laughed.

I didn't tell Aunt Rose it wasn't Eddie who had said that about her. I just smiled and let Eddie have the attention.

"Where's Randall?" Uncle Clyde asked.

"He's feeding the chickens and gathering eggs," Glen said. "He's just about ready. Mom's in the cellar."

That's when we heard Henry and Robert screaming.

"Somethin' terrible has happened to Dad!" We heard Robert yelling as he ran up the steps to the side porch.

Uncle Clyde grabbed the screen door and opened it wide for Robert. "What happened, Robert?" he asked.

Robert was pale and shaking as he spoke. "Dad was in the chicken coop an' then Henry and I heard this terrible thud. When Henry an' I ran t' see what was happenin, chickens were flyin' everywhere an' Dad was lying on the floor in terrible pain. Henry's still with Dad, but Dad can't move. He's in terrible pain!"

Uncle Clyde and Aunt Rose raced quickly down the side steps behind Robert while Eddie and I followed them to the chicken coop. Uncle Clyde opened the small door to the chicken coop and looked in.

"It's my back!" We heard Dad call as he lay helplessly on the chicken coop floor. "Somethin' went out in my back an' I can't get up!"

I peeked into the chicken coop and chickens were squabbling and fluttering everywhere. The musty smell of old straw and dirty chickens was only worsened by the frightened look upon Dad's face.

Uncle Clyde and Aunt Rose bent over to lift Dad while Henry and Robert looked on. *"Don't touch me, yet!"* he cried. He lay on his back while hot beads of sweat rolled off his pale forehead. "It pains terribly! I'm afraid it's somethin' serious. I'm afraid there'll be no fishin' trip this time, boys."

"We're not concerned 'bout our fishin' trip, Dad," Robert said. "We can go fishin' anytime."

With Aunt Rose on one side and Uncle Clyde on the other, Dad painfully wrapped his arms over their shoulders. As they lifted Dad, the pain became more excruciating and his total weight fell upon their shoulders. Suddenly his legs went out from under him as though he were standing on ice and Dad's face twisted into a snarl and he began to cry.

"Don't worry, Randall, we'll get you to the house. Just hang on," Uncle Clyde said.

Slowly, Uncle Clyde and Aunt Rose inched their way to the tiny door and lowered Dad to the earth below. Now, Dad's shirt seeped with sweat. His face became whiter and he lost all sense of strength.

Never before had any of us seen Dad so weakened, so helpless. Almost instantly his strength was tapped from his body and his face seemed old. Always the picture of health and manliness, Dad now became totally dependent on the strength of Aunt Rose and Uncle Clyde. Step by step the pain grew worse as each jolt seemed to drive long knives into Dad's spine.

Finally, they reached the side porch. *"Oh, Lord!"* Mom cried as she met them there and scrambled down the porch steps. *"What is it, Randall? What has happened to you?"*

"It's his back, Lydia. Something went out in his back and he fell to the chicken coop floor," Aunt Rose explained.

"My legs don't want t' respond, Lydia. I don't think I can make it up those steps."

"Then we'll carry you up, Randall. You just relax and put all your weight on us," Mom replied. As she spoke, Mom squeezed her tiny body between Aunt Rose and Dad to give added strength, while Uncle Clyde lifted from the other side. Without saying a word, Roberta held the screen door open and soon Dad was in his bedroom seated on the bed. Perspiration dripped from his body as though he had worked all day in the boiling sun. Carefully, Mom peeled Dad's soaked shirt from his aching body and eased him to a reclining position on the bed below.

For the remainder of the day, Dad lay in bed. There was no movement without agonizing pain. All day he remained pale and weak. Back and forth, Mom went from the kitchen sink to Dad's side with a wet towel. Time and time again, she wiped the sweat from Dad's forehead and ran her fingers through his hair.

"Uncle Clyde and Henry went up to Mr. Pierce's gas station to call Doctor Higgins, Randall," Mom said. She sat at his side, her hands folded gently inside his. With each sharp pain stabbing through his spine, Dad's hands tightened around hers.

"I think it was right t' send them, Lydia," he finally said. "I do believe it might be time t' call the doctor."

Again, the knife-like pain shot through Dad's spine. Dad's body stiffened. He grit his teeth tightly and moaned loudly. Mom ran her fingers through Dad's sweaty hair. "You'll be fine, Randall," she said. With the back of her hand she wiped a tear from Dad's eye. "Doctor Higgins will no doubt give you some pain pills and before you know it, you'll be back to normal." Mom's words came straight from her heart, but her eyes told the truth. Tears fell from her cheeks. She brushed them aside and smiled down at Dad. "I love you, Randall," she said.

It was late afternoon of the next day when Doctor Higgins arrived. Once again he stopped at the side porch, calmly pulled his black satchel from his car, and patted Teddy on the head. Together the two climbed the steps of the side porch.

Once inside, Mom led Doctor Higgins straight to Dad. There was small talk between Doctor Higgins and Dad, and then Doctor Higgins began his examination. First, he took Dad's hands and pulled him to a sitting position. Next, he lifted Dad's arms. Once again sweat began pouring down Dad's face as he grimaced in pain. Then, Doctor Higgins laid Dad carefully down on his back and began pulling on his toes. Outside the bedroom, we children waited anxiously for Doctor Higgins' report.

Finally, Doctor Higgins spoke. "I'm afraid it's very serious, Randall."

Mom sat at the edge of the bed holding Dad's hand. She brushed a tear from his cheek and ran her fingers through his hair.

Dad spoke now. "Just how serious is it, Doctor? I want the truth, so don't hide anythin' from me now. Does it mean I'm goin' t' be confined t' this confounded bed for a few more days? How serious is it?"

Doctor Higgins stood at the foot of the bed and latched his black satchel. He looked down at Dad. "I'm afraid it's much worse than that, Randall. I'm afraid you're going to have to spend some time in the hospital." He lifted his satchel and waited for Dad's reply.

"The hospital?" Dad cried. *"I can't go t' the hospital! I've got crops comin' on. There's still work t' be done in the fields...."* He stopped speaking and looked to Doctor Higgins for sympathy.

Aunt Rose and Uncle Clyde arrived just in time to hear Dad and Doctor Higgins speaking of the hospital. They stood at the threshold of the bedroom door, but said nothing.

"I'm sorry, Randall. You wanted the truth and I'm leveling with you. You have a slipped disc, Randall, and that's serious business." He set his satchel on the foot of the bed and moved directly to

Dad. "You see, Randall, your spine is just like my knuckles. He bent the fingers of each hand and slid them between each other. You can see how the knuckles on my one fist interlocks with the knuckles of the other? Well, your spine is just like this. You have discs like these knuckles and if one of them slips out, like this, (here Doctor Higgins slipped one of his knuckles away from the others) the others come crashing down and this disc can pinch a nerve. That's exactly what's happening with your back right now. That's why you can't move without that disc pinching a nerve in your spine."

Doctor Higgins walked back to the end of the bed and rested his large hands upon the bed railing. "You have no choice, Randall," he continued. "You need medical care that I can't give you here at home."

There was a short pause as Dad took a deep breath. "I tell you I can't go t' the hospital, Doctor. The crops are comin' on an' I've got a job t' go to. I can't miss work. The hospital's out of the question. Do you hear me?" Dad spoke convincingly, but his eyes were asking, once again, for sympathy.

"Now, listen to reason, Randall," Mom said. "Your health is the most important thing to consider here. And don't you worry about the crops. The children are big enough to take care of things. They're hard workers, Randall. You know that. Besides, what good could you do at home if you're in such pain?" She caressed Dad's hand fondly and lifted it to her lips.

Tears began to dampen Dad's eyes. A hush fell upon the room as he turned his head in shame to hide the tears he now fought to control. "The truth is, I'm not much good t' anybody in this condition," he murmured.

"It's not forever, Randall," Doctor Higgins spoke again. "It may require an operation, but we might be able to control the problem with a simple body cast."

Dad turned to face Mom again and squeezed her hand tightly. "I can't believe what I've put you an' the kids through, Lydia. It seems ever since we moved here, t' Anglin' Road, we've been pushed into an uphill battle."

Mom smiled down at Dad. "I wouldn't trade it for the world, Randall, and neither would you."

"First the job, then Glen's illness, now my back. What will it be next?" Dad paused. Then lifting his eyes to meet Mom's he spoke again. "It's been rough on you an' the kids, Lydia, but I swear I'll do better for you someday. I promise."

"Randall, I've never known happiness like I've known here on Anglin' Road. For that matter, none of us have. There isn't a child in this family who hasn't fallen in love with this place. We don't ask for anything else. All we want is for you to get your health back." Mom fought back her own tears now as she bent to kiss Dad on the forehead.

"We'll put you in the hospital tomorrow, Randall," Doctor Higgins said. "You're going to feel quite a bit of pain between now and then, so I'll leave this bottle of pain pills just in case you need them." Doctor Higgins lifted his satchel from Dad's bed and walked to the door. "And by the way, Randall," he spoke as he paused at the bedroom door, "Lydia's right about this family of yours. I don't think you'll need to worry about a thing while you're recuperating." He reached down and lightly pinched Roberta's cheek.

28 | "Good ol' Aunt Rose!"

After careful examination in Sharon General Hospital, Doctor Higgins decided Dad would not need an operation at this time. When Mom heard those words she wept once again, for joy.

However, the first few days in the hospital were just as painful as the day Dad's disc slipped in his spine. For three days he lay flat on his back and could not turn right or left. Several pounds of weight were attached to his legs and arranged on pulleys so the weight would pull his legs at the base of his back, thus relieving some of the pressure from the slipped disc. Hopefully, in a few days, the disc would slide back into its proper place.

After a few more days the weights were removed, but Dad still could not walk. The pain was still excruciating and Dad finally accepted the fact that proper healing of his back would not be accomplished in mere days. He would be handicapped for weeks, perhaps months.

One morning Doctor Higgins came into Dad's hospital room. At the foot of the bed he lifted Dad's feet and began to massage them one at a time. "I want to see if you're getting proper circulation, Randall," he said. Satisfied that Dad's circulation was good, Doctor Higgins stepped to the side of the bed. "We're going to get you on your feet today, Randall. It's going to pain some, but I want you to get your muscles and circulation up to par, because in a couple of days we're going to put a body cast on you and hopefully send you home."

"Home!" Dad's eyes became aglow.

"Remember now, that cast will be here to hold your spine in place, and I'll not have you lifting or even walking much for some time. It will be weeks before you'll be able to lift or work." Doctor Higgins looked to Mom now and spoke with authority. "It will be up to you, Lydia, to see that he follows my instructions. He must not abuse that back. If it doesn't heal properly now it could mean surgery the next time he's back here."

"It'll be rough keeping him down, Doctor, but we'll manage. Somehow we'll keep him down if we have to tie him to his bed," Mom asserted with a smile.

A long pause followed Mom's words as though both she and Doctor Higgins were waiting for Dad's response. Finally, Dad braced himself on the edge of the bed and looked Doctor Higgins in the eyes. "I promise I'll do what you suggest, Doctor. Just get this cast on me an' show me the way home. It's been nearly three weeks since I've been with the kids." Dad chuckled and smiled to Mom. "I suppose they've got the ol' homestead torn apart by now."

"Now that's one thing you don't have to worry about, Randall. Rose and Clyde are with them, as they have been throughout this whole ordeal." She walked to the window and looked down at the passing cars on State Street, below. "You know Rose is keeping them in line. Lord knows she's bent Henry's ear a dozen times already!" Mom laughed.

"God bless Uncle Clyde an' Aunt Rose!" Dad grinned in return. "What would we ever do without them?"

"I often wonder that myself," Mom said. "You know, I think they kind of like raisin' that 'brood' of ours!"

"God have pity on them!" Dad smiled.

Soon, the day arrived for Dad's cast to be put on. First, Doctor Higgins slipped a long, gauze tubing that looked much like a T-shirt carefully over Dad's neck and slid it over his body until it neatly covered every inch that was to be plastered. Next, he took long, thin wrappings of cloth and dipped them into a pan of wet plaster and slowly began wrapping these neatly over the gauze covering. Piece by piece, Doctor Higgins wrapped the cloth around Dad. Beginning at the neck, he slowly worked his way down to Dad's waist.

Finally, after two hours, Dad's cast was completed. When finished, his cast was nearly an inch thick and now resembled a metal suit of armor worn by knights of medieval time. Now, the cast must harden. In two days, Dad would go home.

In the morning, Doctor Higgins came into Dad's room and thumped on the cast with his bare knuckles. "Sounds good—looks hard," he uttered. "How's it feel, Randall?"

"Strange, Doctor, very strange. In fact it's so tight 'round my stomach I'm havin' difficulties breathin', Doctor."

"Too tight, huh?" Doctor Higgins thumped on Dad's stomach. "Well, there are two solutions to a problem like this, Randall. One is to not eat anymore so your stomach will shrink, or we can go the other route and cut a hole in the cast so your stomach can stick out some and you'll be free to breathe again. It's not a common practice, but we can bend a little here."

"Perhaps we'd better try the latter, Doctor," Dad insisted with a loud laugh. "I enjoy eatin' too much t' try the first idea."

Doctor Higgins left the room for a short period of time. "I think we have just the right ticket for a job like this," he said as he reentered the room carrying another black satchel. Digging into the satchel, he pulled out a tool that looked like a vibrating knife with no teeth. He plugged the long wire, dangling from its end, into an electrical outlet while Dad sat at the edge of the bed, waiting anxiously to breathe freely once again.

Doctor Higgins turned the vibrating tool on and pressed it against the plaster encircling Dad's stomach. Around Dad's stomach, Doctor Higgins began cutting a wide circle as big as a basketball. At the end of the circle the plaster fell to the floor and out popped Dad's belly like a balloon being filled with a sudden burst of air.

Dad stood up and sucked in a large gulp of fresh air. Slowly letting the air out, he chuckled sheepishly. "Looks silly," he said. "But it does the job!"

The next morning Uncle Clyde and Aunt Rose went to the hospital to pick Dad up and bring him home. When Uncle Clyde's car pulled up the long driveway we all waited anxiously as the car door opened and Dad carefully set his feet to the ground. His face was no longer pale. Instead of tears, there was a sparkle in his deep brown eyes. "Home sweet home!" he said as Aunt Rose and Uncle Clyde lifted him from the car.

"Welcome home, Randall," Mom said. Caressing his hand tightly, she kissed Dad on the lips.

Wesley stood beside Dad. Then backing away, he put his hands to his mouth and burst into laughter. "You look like our potbelly stove, Dad, wit' dat hole in your stomach!"

Uncle Clyde's belly shook with laughter. "By golly, you do at that, Randall!" He stepped back to get a better look at Dad's belly hanging out of the cast. Then he laughed louder and pulled his pants up with his wrists.

Dad blushed and lifting his chin to the blue sky above, he took a deep breath and said, "It sure is good t' be home. There's somethin' medicinal about this place." He took another deep breath and the strong scent of freshly cooked corn on the cob tickled his nose. "Who wants t' bet I could eat fifteen ears right now?" he boasted. "No takers, huh? Not even you, Henry?" Dad winked remembering the last time Henry tried to eat fifteen ears in one setting. Two days later, he was still sick and vowed he would never eat another ear of corn as long as he lived.

Uncle Clyde and Aunt Rose helped Dad up the steps of the side porch and into the house. This time there was no pain, no twisting of his face and no sweat boiling down his face. Only a smile was on his lips as he settled into a kitchen chair and took a long sigh. "What have you all been up to while I was away on vacation, anyhow?" he asked.

"Uncle Clyde and Aunt Rose have been keepin' us real busy, Dad," I spoke up. I looked proudly to Uncle Clyde and Uncle Clyde winked back.

"They have, have they?" Dad smiled to Uncle Clyde and Uncle Clyde returned another wink. "How are the fields, boys? The corn an' tomatoes ready t' can, I suppose. How about the cabbage an' the potatoes?"

"All the cannin's done, Dad," Roberta proudly boasted. "We told you Uncle Clyde and Aunt Rose have kept us busy."

"Lord sakes, is she tellin' the truth, Clyde?" Dad asked with searching eyes.

"Nearly all done, Randall. We haven't touched the potatoes, of course, but that's comin' next week. We've still got plenty of corn to take into town, yet. And, we're going to have more tomatoes comin' on, so Rose wants to make more ketchup," Uncle Clyde declared. "Oh, yes, I nearly forgot about the sauerkraut! I wasn't sure how much salt to put on top, so I thought I'd wait till you got home."

Dad stared at Uncle Clyde momentarily, and then dropping his eyes to the floor he shook his head in disbelief. Once again his eyes began to fill with tears. "No one ever had truer friends than you an' Rose," he spoke now as he looked Uncle Clyde in the eyes.

"Enough of that mushy talk, Randall!" Aunt Rose interrupted as she stepped between the two men and pulled Dad to his feet. "Good Lord, you'd think we did something special the way you act! Three weeks in the hospital and you start acting like city folk! Besides that, the kids did all the work anyways. And right now you need to get to your bedroom and rest your body. Ridin' down Anglin' Road couldn't have helped your back none."

With Aunt Rose on one side of Dad and Mom on the other, the two women slowly guided Dad to his bedroom. "Those kids of ours are growin' up, Randall," Aunt Rose continued to lecture to Dad while Mom smiled with pride. "I tell you they sure are workers. Oh, it wasn't all downhill, I assure you. Occasionally I had to box their ears. But on the whole they worked like silly little fools. Even Wesley! That little rascal! I had to take the belt to him once or twice, but by golly I straightened him up in a hurry! No little brat's gonna tell me to 'go climb a tree!' By golly, I tanned his little bottom! You can bet on that!"

Dad laughed at the thought of Wesley being bold enough to tell Aunt Rose to 'go climb a tree!' But, more important, he was proud of Aunt Rose. He could count on Aunt Rose to keep a firm hand on all his children. But he knew, as we all did, the real reason she was talking so much was to keep him from praising Uncle Clyde and her for doing what they enjoyed, taking care of the 'brood.'

Once in bed, Dad asked about Glen and the girls. "Are they ready for the musical? What songs will they sing? Is Glen feeling well?"

Yes, Glen was feeling well. Yes, they were ready for the musical. And the songs they would sing were "Whispering Hope" and "It Is No Secret".

After supper Uncle Clyde and Aunt Rose talked with Dad in his bedroom for awhile and then they went home, promising to get more work done tomorrow.

That evening, after we children had retired to our bedrooms, we could faintly hear Mom and Dad speaking in their bedroom below.

"They truly are special, ya know, Lydia; Rose an' Clyde, I mean," we heard Dad say.

"They certainly are," Mom agreed. She spoke softly and proudly.

"You never told me they were here pickin' an' cannin' the crops, Lydia."

"Well, you know Rose, Randall. She wouldn't hear of me telling you about it. She knew if you found out about it your pride would have gotten you up and out of that hospital bed and home to do your share long before you should have."

Upstairs, I lay in bed and thought of Aunt Rose and Uncle Clyde. How I longed for the day Dad could take the heavy cast from his body and somehow repay them for all the good they had done for our family.

Henry lifted the kerosene lamp from the tall dresser, blew across the top, snuffing the golden flames and set it back upon the dresser.

"Sure is good t' have Dad home again," Robert said as he jumped across the foot of the bed and landed beside me.

"Sure is," we all chorused together.

"Did anyone tell Mom 'bout Aunt Rose chasin' that man away yesterday?" I asked.

"No. And if you know what's good for you you'll never mention it again either!" Esther called from the girls' bedroom. "Some things are better left unsaid and that's one of them." She chuckled.

Now I burst into a big smile as I proudly thought of Aunt Rose standing there, in the driveway, swinging that broom wildly at that mean man as he jumped into his car and sped down the driveway.

"I'll bet it was that same man who asked all the questions down by the bridge that day when we were fishin'," Robert said.

"I'm sure it was, the way Aunt Rose described him. Too bad we were in school. I'd like t' have seen that!" Henry spoke with laughter trickling from his voice. "It makes me angry, but I still have t' laugh at Aunt Rose."

"Serves him right," I said. "Imagine that! Suggesting that Glen be put in a home for crippled children because it's too much of a problem for Mom with eight children an' Dad with a slipped disc!"

"Who's he t' tell anybody what they should or shouldn't do?" Robert asked.

"What a terrible thought!" Roberta joined in with a tone that told me she was crying. "Don't adults understand what life is all about? How can anybody in their right mind stoop so low as to think Mom could ever let any of her children go to a home? Why is Glen any different from us just because he can't walk? How terrible!"

"If Mom ever knew someone suggested puttin' Glen in a nursing home it would surely break her heart," Henry said sadly.

"If Dad eber knew—he'd kill dem, I betcha!" Wesley murmured.

"Oh, Wesley! He wouldn't kill them, either!" Eddie broke in. "He'd be pretty upset. But he wouldn't go kill nobody."

"Betcha he would," Wesley murmured once again from under the covers.

"Let's all promise we'll never repeat it again, 'cause if it ever got back to Mom or Glen they would surely die," Esther offered.

"I promise," said Eddie.

"So do I," we all agreed.

After all was quiet for awhile, I spoke again with a chuckle in my voice. "Good ol' Aunt Rose!" I said. "Maybe the rest of the world don't understand us an' the way we live here on Anglin' Road, but Aunt Rose sure does!"

29 | Pastor Wiggins

"He's here again, Esther."

"Who's here again?" Esther asked. She lifted herself from her chair and joined me at the kitchen window.

"That man that Aunt Rose chased away the other day! At least he's the man that was askin' all the questions down by the bridge that day." I pushed myself away from the kitchen window and spoke directly to her. "He's in one car an' there's someone else in the car in front of him."

"Let me get a better look," Esther said. She went to the screen door and looked out. Roberta rose from her chair and joined Esther at the door. Together, they pushed the screen door open and stepped to the side porch. "My goodness! It's Pastor Wiggins! That's who's in the first car!" Esther said.

"See what I mean, Pastor," the stranger said as he left his car and joined Pastor Wiggins. He planted his foot firmly on Pastor Wiggins' running board. "There are six more just like those two on the porch. And one of them is crippled!"

The two men began their walk toward the house. Pastor Wiggins paused and smiled at King Tut squabbling and chasing another chicken in the chicken yard. He seemed inattentive as the other man continued to talk.

"And just look at this place! It should have been condemned long ago. I'm telling you, Pastor, they don't even have electricity here!"

Pastor Wiggins continued to ignore the small man. While the man continued to ramble, Pastor Wiggins's attention was drawn to the two girls standing on the porch. At the moment he had not recognized them as Esther and Roberta. He took his hat from his head and wiped the inside lining with his hanky. He stood tall, nearly six foot tall. His hair was black and his nose long. But he was a handsome gentleman in his late twenties. His gray suit hung loose upon his broad frame and there was a strong resemblance to the famous evangelist, Billy Graham.

"Esther! Roberta! Well, I'll be! Heaven's sakes! I didn't know you lived here!" He smiled for the first time, plopped his hat upon his head and hurried to the two girls who were rushing down the steps to meet him. "So, this is where you two live. My goodness!" He pulled the two girls close to him and embraced them excitedly. Esther and Roberta hung tightly to his arms and blushed.

I stepped to the side porch and jumped down beside the other man's car. Henry, Robert, and Wesley were playing basketball in front of the barn, but when they saw the two strangers they quickly stopped and ran to the side porch. I knew that Henry and Robert had already recognized the smaller man because each had a scowl, but said nothing.

At the screen door, Teddy now paced back and forth, whimpering, while Eddie pushed the door open and wheeled Glen to his favorite spot on the side porch.

"Pastor, this is no time to be getting friendly. Remember, we came here on business." The stranger almost whispered his words.

"Mr. Farnsworth!" Pastor Wiggins said sharply. He spun his head around to face the small man. "We came here because you asked me to meet a family who lived in an old house with no electricity. That's exactly what I'm doing, I'll thank you!"

"I think you can see for yourself, Pastor, that this place isn't fit for children!"

Pastor Wiggins spoke angrily now. "Mr. Farnsworth, I'll thank you to keep your remarks to yourself, if you please! We're in the company of two young ladies now, and I'll not hear another word about it!"

Mr. Farnsworth backed away, fidgeting nervously with his hat.

From behind Mr. Farnsworth's car I could hear the entire conversation between Mr. Farnsworth and Pastor Wiggins. I could feel my face becoming hotter and hotter, like it did that day Henry told me what this man was up to. I was madder than a mad dog! When Mr. Farnsworth wasn't looking, I sneaked to the opposite side of his car. Nobody could see me from there. Inside me I kept hearing a voice saying, "Do it! Do it!" And I became madder and madder. Bending to the ground, my heart began to beat louder and louder. My nervous hands became sweaty. I picked up a small stick from the edge of the driveway and poked it into the valve of Mr. Farnsworth's back tire. At first there was a loud, 'sssssss' sound as the air began to rapidly seep from the tire. Then, as if from heaven, a gust of wind kicked up whirling twigs across the yard, drowning the sound of the air leaving the tire. Mr. Farnsworth paced back and forth beside the car, twisting his hat nervously with both hands.

I knew Mom would not be happy if she saw me do this. But I thought of Aunt Rose, now. "Sometimes ya gotta do somethin' bad to be good!" she once told me. 'If she could see me now, she would be mighty proud of me,' I thought.

Like an exalted king, I listened to the warm air seep from that tire—like an angry snake, hissing at an unwanted visitor. When at last the final tinge of air had completely escaped from that tire, I looked to heaven. Joyful tears began to trickle down my cheeks. Somewhere in the distance, I knew some sweet choir was softly singing, Hallelujah! Hallelujah! I tossed the long, thin stick into the weeds, behind me, and quietly joined the others at the side porch, as though I had never left.

"So, you're Pastor Wiggins!" Dad said as he hobbled down the porch steps with Mom at his side. "The girls have told us a lot about you. Pleased t' meet you!" Dad shook Pastor Wiggins's hand firmly. "This is my wife, Lydia."

"It is indeed my honor, I assure you." Pastor Wiggins shook Mom's hand. "Your daughters bear a strong resemblance to you, Mrs. Stevenson."

"I'm honored as well, Pastor. Thank you."

Pastor Wiggins stared at Dad's stomach momentarily. "Pardon me for staring, Mr. Stevenson, but your daughters told me about your cast." He laughed. "They even told me about Wesley saying you look like a potbellied stove. If I may say so, I see what he means!" He laughed louder this time as Dad patted his protruding stomach and laughed with him.

The laughter continued while Mom quietly slipped to the side porch. "Would you like to meet Wesley and the rest of the family, Pastor?" she asked.

"It would be an honor."

"I'm sorry, Pastor," Mom apologized, as Pastor Wiggins approached the side porch. "We didn't meet your friend, yet. He's welcome to join us."

"Oh, I'm not sure he's feeling so well right now. Anyhow, he's not the sociable type," the pastor spoke softly and laughed again. "And this is Glen!" he said as he reached across the side porch and shook Glen's hand. "My goodness! I've heard so much about you, young man. You can't be as talented as your sisters brag about, can you?"

"Any talents I have, Pastor, I truly thank the Lord."

"Wonderful!" Pastor Wiggins uttered. "Simply wonderful!"

"Pastor," Mr. Farnsworth began to speak. "Pastor, I'd like to speak to you in privacy, if I may."

Pulling the pastor aside, Mr. Farnsworth began to speak. "Pastor, I asked that we speak alone. Could you ask these two girls to leave for a moment?" He gave a mean look to Esther and Roberta who were once again gathered in Pastor Wiggins's arms.

"I don't like secrets, Mr. Farnsworth. What you have to say, you can say in front of them." Pastor Wiggins stood taller now and looked down on Mr. Farnsworth with a scowl.

Mr. Farnsworth began to point his finger up to Pastor Wiggins's nose and then changed his mind. Timidly, he spoke. "Pastor, may I remind you these people don't even go to church!"

Pastor Wiggins' face became red. "Mr. Farnsworth, do you have a garage?" he asked with a stern look upon his face.

Puzzled by such a question, Mr. Farnsworth paused with a blank look upon his face. "Why of course I have a garage!" he finally answered. "What does that have to do with anything?"

"Mr. Farnsworth," Pastor Wiggins looked him straight in the eyes, "just because you walk into your garage it doesn't make you a car, does it? Lord sakes! We have people who walk into our church and that doesn't make them Christians! These people don't go to church and they just beam with Christian love!"

Pastor Wiggins excused himself from Mr. Farnsworth and walked back to the side porch where we had all assembled. "You know, Mr. and Mrs. Stevenson," Pastor Wiggins said, "whatever you folks are doing down here on Anglin' Road, it's right. Why, if I could bring all the young people of our church down here, I believe they'd all grow up to be beautiful citizens and hard workers. I've never seen so much love and respect in one place in all my life!"

"Pastor, may I remind you of something," Mr. Farnsworth interrupted and pulled Pastor Wiggins aside. "You know I give a considerable amount of my tithe to your church," I heard him say.

"If need be, I'm sure the Community church wouldn't mind if I pulled my letter and joined them."

Pastor Wiggins smiled in return. "Mr. Farnsworth, I see nothing but love in this home. I think we can all learn a lesson here. And by the way, from what I understand, the Community church would welcome you with open arms. I understand they're still looking for the same type people we Methodist are - *sinners!*"

Dad was now sitting on the side porch steps beside Teddy. When he heard Pastor Wiggins say that the Community church would welcome Mr. Farnsworth because they're looking for sinners, too, he smothered his laughter and slapped his knees. "By golly, Teddy, that's my kind of preacher!" he whispered.

Mr. Farnsworth spun around and nearly ran back to his car. His face was steaming. With no more questions, he jumped into his car and sped backwards down the driveway to Anglin' Road.

Thump! Thump! Thump! I heard the flat tire slap angrily at Anglin' Road as the car limped toward the wooden bridge. Mr. Farnsworth jumped out of his car and kicked the back tire. Then, crawling back into his car, he slammed the driver's door. Slowly, he hobbled past the bridge and toward Hartford.

Dad heard the commotion and peeked around the corner of the house where he could see Mr. Farnsworth. A wide grin spread across his face. He turned and winked to me. I don't know how, but I think he knew.

That's when Henry jumped off the side porch. His face was red with anger. "That's him! That's him!" he shouted. "That's the man who hurt Betty Jane! I jist recognized his car! I remember him now speeding past me that day I stood on the bridge. I remember him hidin' his face as he went by. I remember his hat, too! But I remember that car from the time he stopped on the bridge and made us real mad! That's him! That's him!"

Pastor Wiggins turned sharply to Henry. "Are you sure what you're saying, young man?"

"Yes, I'm sure! I'm as sure as the nose on my face! That's the man who sped by me the day Betty Jane was hurt!"

"Let's go get him," Dad shouted and headed for the car.

"No, Mr. Stevenson! I think I have a better idea. He's not going anywhere. He thinks nobody will ever know the harm he did to Betty Jane. That's why he was bold enough to come down here today." Then Pastor Wiggins turned and smiled as he placed his hat on his head. "I'll stop by and see Constable Snyder when I leave here. He'll know exactly what to do."

Pastor Wiggins gave Esther and Roberta a hug before he stepped into his car. Waving goodbye to all of us, he smiled as he shouted back to Glen on the side porch. "You take care of yourself, young man. And good luck in that musical." Then he drove down Anglin' Road and soon was out of sight.

The next day Constable Snyder stopped at our house. He shook each of our hands then smiled. "I think Mr. Farnsworth won't be bothering you for some time," he said. "I think he's going to be busy minding his own business for awhile." Then he smiled and waved good-bye, as he slapped his hat against his knee and drove down Anglin' Road.

Sunday morning, Mom called us all together in the kitchen.

"Get your best clothes on, children. We're going to church! Your dad finally found a minister he says is true to the bone!"

We were late. But what a happy moment for Pastor Wiggins and the whole congregation as Henry pushed Glen down the aisle to the front pew. Behind them were Mom and Dad, Wesley, Esther, Roberta, Robert, Eddie, and then me.

Pastor Wiggins stood behind the pulpit and broke into a wide grin. For a moment he thumbed through the pages of his hymnal.

Then, he looked to the pianist and smiled. "Let's all stand and sing hymn number twenty-nine," he said.

In front of us the pianist turned a few pages of her hymnal and smiled in return. We lifted our hymnals while her fingers began to come down hard upon the keys of the piano. Pastor Wiggins winked to Mom and we began to sing:

> "When peace, like a river, at-tend-eth my way,
> When sorrows like sea—bil-lows roll;
> What-ev—er my lot, Thou has taught me to say,
> 'It is well, it is well with my soul'
> It is well—with my soul,
> It is well, it is well with my soul."

30 | The Musical

Hartford's school gymnasium was dimly lit. A total of eight light bulbs hung down from the ceiling. Each light bulb was encased in a glass bowl that resembled a frosted fish bowl. A thousand birthday candles could have given the same amount of candlepower. Two hundred-fifty wooden chairs were arranged on the gymnasium floor facing the tiny stage. Early arrivers began filling these seats. Another two hundred people began packing the bleachers, directly behind these seats.

Colorful red and white crepe paper streamers stretched across the ceiling and down the walls. Large pictures of the cast dangled from these walls. The sweet aroma of hot chocolate, coffee, and popcorn drifted in from the hallway where temporary concession stands now sat.

In the hall, behind the stage, performers began running helter-skelter, as though one emergency quickly followed another. Excited people began rushing to selected seats. Friends who had not seen each other for some time began milling around, talking about the big event. Others were searching for friends and family.

All the pomp and ceremony of the great Roman Circuses could not compare with the splendor of this gala event. Tonight was Hartford's grand musical!

On the gymnasium floor, directly in front of the stage, members of a miniature orchestra began tuning their instruments.

"We're lucky to get seats so close to the stage," Mom said to Aunt Rose as she squeezed down the third row and sat directly in front of the stage. "We'll be able to see Glen and the girls real well from here."

"I just hope we don't make them nervous with the entire brood sitting so close," Aunt Rose said. Then she looked down the long row of seats we nearly filled. "You boys behave now and don't do anything to distract Glen and the girls. You hear me?"

"Believe it or not, Aunt Rose, we're just as excited as you and Mom are," Robert said. "We'll behave."

Aunt Rose stretched across Uncle Clyde's empty seat and snapped Robert on the ear with her index finger. "Just see that you do!" Turning to Mom, she said, "Land sakes you're getting all fidgety, Lydia! Why don't you sit still?"

"I guess I am a little nervous," Mom agreed. "But it is almost time to begin and I don't see Grandma and Uncle Slim yet. What do you suppose has happened to them?"

"They're probably having trouble finding a parking place, Lydia. Good Lord! You know this place is packed. Don't worry about it! Clyde's waitin' at the door to usher them in as soon as they get here."

"Just the same, I'll feel much better when they do arrive."

"Well, wait no longer! Here they come now. My goodness! I don't believe I ever saw Grandma shuffle so fast in all her life. You would think this was an important event in her life. My Lord, just look at her!"

Grandma hurriedly squeezed past Henry and Robert with Uncle Clyde and Uncle Slim close behind. "Nearly didn't make it," she complained softly to Mom and Aunt Rose. "I kept tellin' Slim to hurry, but he insisted we had plenty of time."

"Well, thank goodness, you did make it on time. That's all that matters," Mom assured her.

"Did Ned and Carol and all their kids make it yet?" Grandma asked.

"Yes. In fact, Uncle Robert and Aunt Rachel are here, way in the back. Samuel and Maxine are here, and Margaret and Harry are here with all their kids."

"Good golly!" Uncle Clyde blurted out. "Look who just walked through the door! It's Larry Vincent and his wife!"

"Well, Lord sakes!" Aunt Rose exclaimed. "If that don't take the cake! Go tell them they can sit here, beside us, Clyde. Henry and Robert won't mind givin' up their seats - would you boys?"

"No, Ma'am! We sure wouldn't, Aunt Rose," Henry said as he and Robert rose from their seats and scooted down the aisle.

Uncle Clyde rushed to greet Larry and Alice. Someone in the crowd recognized Larry and shouted, "Hey, that's Larry Vincent of 'Pillow Talk'!" For a moment all became unusually quiet as the crowd seemed to focus on Larry and Alice Vincent.

"I'm sorry we're late," Larry apologized. He shook Dad's hand and then gently helped Alice take her coat off and looped it over the back of her seat.

Suddenly, the lights began to slowly dim and my stomach took flip-flops. At precisely eight o'clock the red, velvet curtains were pulled open and silence fell over the crowd.

At the far corner of the stage, Glen sat proudly in his wheel-chair. He smiled and looked down at Mom. He was handsome in his black suit and red tie. I was so proud of Glen I wanted to cry. But I didn't. I just took a deep breath and looked down the row at Mom and Dad, Aunt Rose and Uncle Clyde, and Grandma and Uncle Slim. Oh, how proud they all looked!

In the middle of the stage, sitting on a high throne, was a tall, handsome young man dressed in a stunning white suit with long tails. On his head was a tall, white, stovepipe hat that reminded me of the tall black hat Abraham Lincoln always wore. Mom said the handsome young man was the interlocutor. The young girls in the audience giggled and whispered at the sight of this splendid figure. Older girls swooned and blushed.

Directly behind the handsome interlocutor were the remaining cast and chorus. On each side of the stage were seated three, colorful hillbillies. Each was holding a tambourine and as the curtain opened each began shaking his tambourine in unison.

The tiny orchestra blared a loud introduction. The entire cast stood up and suddenly the gymnasium was filled with a song of welcome.

When it ended, the handsome interlocutor stepped down from his throne and once again the young girls swooned.

"Mr. Jackson Johnston," he called.

From the left side of the stage, one of the colorful, exuberant hillbillies jumped from his seat and took a couple of bows. A large, hillbilly hat was planted awkwardly on his head and nearly covered his eyes. Baggy pants held by long suspenders drooped to the floor. A small tattered jacket was buttoned tightly to his chest. Smudges of dirt spotted his face and two of his front teeth were missing.

He smiled at the audience, did a perfect cartwheel, then put his hands to his lips and began blowing kisses to the audience. Grandma began to laugh and shake at the same time.

Finally, the hillbilly shook his tambourine and strolled lazily toward the interlocutor.

"Why that's Roberta!" Mom whispered to Aunt Rose.

"For heaven's sakes! It is!" Aunt Rose said.

"Mr. Jackson Johnston!" the interlocutor shouted above the laughter of the audience.

"Yes, sire!" said Mr. Jackson Johnston. He paused and gave a wide smile to the audience. His eyes rolled in his head. With his nose in the air and his hat held high above his head, Mr. Jackson

Johnston wriggled his hat in one hand and shook his tambourine in the other and then strolled lazily back to his seat and sat down.

Puzzled, the interlocutor called across the stage to Mr. Jackson Johnston.

"Mr. Jackson Johnston!" the interlocutor repeated his call. "Mr. Johnston Jackson, over here (pointing to the opposite side of the stage), tells me that you are quite a fisherman."

Mr. Jackson Johnston stood up once again, bowed to the audience, took another cartwheel, strolled to the center of the stage, and shook his tambourine. The other hillbillies, along the sides of the stage, stood in unison and shook their tambourines.

"He's funny!" I whispered to Eddie and held my stomach.

"Yes, sire, that is correct!" Mr. Jackson Johnston said.

"Would you mind telling us about your fishing experiences?" the handsome interlocutor asked.

"No, sire, I wouldn't mind telling you at all," Mr. Jackson Johnston said. Once again, Roberta drew back her lips and flashed her toothless smile. Turning her back to the audience, she bent over and flipped the tails of her jacket. Raising her tambourine high above her head she shook her wrist, rambled back to her seat, and sat down to the thunderous roar of the audience.

Dad shook with joy. Uncle Clyde slapped his knee and cackled as though he had the hiccups.

Bewildered, the handsome interlocutor called once again. "Mr. Jackson Johnston!"

"Yes, sire!" Mr. Jackson Johnston said as he rose from his chair, shook his tambourine, and smiled to the audience.

"Mr. Jackson Johnston," the interlocutor declared with a puzzled look on his face. "You were going to tell us about your fishing experiences and then you sat down and forgot to tell us about them!"

Mr. Jackson Johnston gave a blank look; first to the interlocutor and then to the audience. He removed his hat from his head and scratched above the temple. "I did?" he asked.

Once again, he rolled his eyes and flashed a smile to the audience.

Ha! Ha! Ha! The audience laughed harder.

"That's right! You sure did!" the interlocutor assured him.

Once again Mr. Jackson Johnston looked bewildered. He lifted his hat from his head and scratched above his temple. Looking to the audience with a blank expression across his face and then back to the interlocutor he said, "I sure did what, sire?"

Now the others on the stage stood and shook their tambourines.

"Mr. Jackson Johnston," the interlocutor said, almost disgustedly. "Do you have a problem remembering things?"

"Yes, sire, I sure do!" Mr. Jackson Johnston said. Roberta smiled to the audience and flipped her tails.

The interlocutor was indignant now. "Just how long has this been going on, Mr. Jackson Johnston?" he shouted, a bit perturbed.

Roberta looked to the audience with a questionable look.

"How long's what been going on, sire?" she blurted back.

Older men began slapping their knees while elbowing the people beside them. Younger men began stomping their feet and laughing harder. And young and older women held their hands to their lips as if to suppress such inappropriate laughter.

"Who is that funny man up there?" Grandma asked Aunt Rose. "He sure is hilarious!"

"Why, didn't you hear Lydia tell me? It's Roberta!"

"Roberta? Our Roberta?" Grandma looked surprised. "Well, for heaven's sakes! I didn't know she could carry on like that! Why, she's as good as any of those ol' actors in the movies!"

Roberta strolled back to her seat, smiled to the audience, bowed and shook her tambourine. A chorus of other tambourines chimed in while a thunderous ovation rang throughout the gymnasium. Finally, she plopped into her seat, waved her tambourine high above her head, and shook it vigorously.

The interlocutor stepped to the front of the stage and called Bobby Molnar, a young boy about my age, to the stage. Dressed in a sailor's suit Bobby skimmed across the stage and planted himself directly in front of Eddie and me. The music director waved his baton and the small orchestra began playing "I'd Love to Get You On a Slow Boat to China." Bobby began to tap dance.

"Wow! He's terrific!" Dad whispered to Mom.

Grandma smiled and whispered something into Aunt Rose's ear.

"He's a sissy!" I whispered to Eddie.

"He sure is!" Eddie agreed. "Just look at the make-up on his face!"

"If I had the money, I'd put him on a slow boat t' China!" I said to Eddie, and then we both snickered.

As the applause for Bobby Molnar ended, Mr. Jackson Johnston took another bow and smiled to the audience. The tambourines shook and chimed in unison. The interlocutor came forward and introduced a fine looking southern gentleman to the audience. He, too, was dressed in a white suit. Upon his head was a southern gentleman's white hat.

"What song would you like me to sing, Mr. Interlocutor?" the southern gentleman asked.

Now the interlocutor seemed to have lost something and was searching diligently through his pockets. "Do you know where my handkerchief went to?" he asked the southern gentleman as he continued his search through his pockets.

"No, sire, I sure don't," the southern gentleman quipped and flashed a wide smile to the audience. "But if you'll just hum a bar or two maybe I could sing it for you!"

Once again, laughter erupted from the audience. The interlocutor gave a bewildered look to the audience and stopped his search for his missing handkerchief. The southern gentleman stepped to the microphone and when all was quiet he said, "And now, my version of 'That Lucky Old Sun.'"

This song was about a person who wanted to be like the sun and just roll around heaven all day. When the southern gentleman ended his song and stepped back from the microphone, Aunt Rose turned to Uncle Clyde and said, "That's one of my favorite songs. He did a terrific piece of singin', I'll tell you!"

"Look! That's Ronny comin' up, now," I whispered to Eddie. "He's dressed like an ol' hillbilly, too!"

Ronny staggered lazily across the stage while the interlocutor waited patiently. Suspenders held Ronny's long baggy pants to his narrow shoulders. In his left hand he held a large jug that seemed too heavy to carry. His shoulders were slouched and he seemed to be inebriated as each step he took forward was followed by two steps sideways or three backwards. A tall hillbilly hat was pulled down, over his ears. When he reached the interlocutor, Ronny stopped and almost fell over from drunkenness. "Which way to New York?" he slurred. Suddenly, without warning, Ronny's suspenders snapped loose and his pants fell to the floor.

"My goodness!" Grandma blushed as Ronny stood dumbfounded in his red, flannel underwear.

Laughter erupted loudly from the audience and echoed off the walls. Aunt Rose looked weak from laughing and blotted her eyes with a tiny hanky. Dad shook until I thought his cast would crack and fall to pieces.

Ronny tried to pull his pants up, but each time his pants got to his hips his suspenders snapped loose and down came his pants again.

"Here, Ronny! Try these!" someone in the front row hollered. He stood up and threw his suspenders to the stage.

That's when a very fat man beside Eddie stood up and shouted, "If that don't work, try my belt!" He poked his thumb under his belt and the crowd laughed louder.

Finally, with the help of the kind interlocutor, Ronny succeeded in fastening his suspenders and pants in their proper places, and as the audience began to quiet down, the interlocutor asked Ronny to croon his favorite tune.

Ronny stepped to the microphone. A hush fell upon the audience. I sat anxiously waiting, as Ronny loosened his bow tie and looked the audience in the eye. Suddenly, his powerful voice filled the air and I became entranced and hypnotized by Ronny's magical spell. How poised and confident he seemed as he stood center stage and sang so beautifully!

> "When they begin the Beguine
> It brings back the sound of music so tender,
> It brings back the night of tropical splendor,
> It brings back a memory ever green.
> I'm with you once more under the stars
> And down by the shore an orchestra's playing
> When they begin the Beguine…"

At the end of Ronny's song the audience rose to its feet and clapped long and hard. Ronny took a bow and returned to his seat among the other performers.

Once again, the interlocutor stepped to the center of the stage. He winked to Mom below. "And now, ladies and gentlemen," he began, "it gives me great pleasure in presenting to you, the one and only *Lovegood Trio!*"

Mom wriggled nervously in her seat. Aunt Rose slipped her hand over Mom's. Patting it gently, she smiled to Mom. Now, there was a stillness I had not noticed before that hovered over the audience. Esther rose from her seat in the chorus and walked to Glen. Grasping the back of his wheelchair, she pushed him to the center of the stage. Roberta set her tambourine on her seat and followed Esther and Glen.

There was a moment's pause as the two girls took their positions beside Glen. Not a sound could be heard in the entire auditorium. People who normally whispered were now staring, waiting anxiously. My palms became sweaty. I held my breath while my heart pounded like a drum inside my chest.

Glen smiled and nodded to the orchestra leader below the stage. Then they began:

> "Soft as the voice of an angel,
> Breathing a lesson unheard,
> Hope, with a gentle persuasion,
> Whispers her comforting word.
> Whispering Hope, Oh, how welcome thy voice,
> Making my heart in its sorrow rejoice.
> Wait, till the darkness is over,
> Wait, till the tempest is done,
> Hope for the sunshine tomorrow,
> After the shower is gone.
> Whispering Hope, Oh, how welcome thy voice,
> Making my heart in its sorrow rejoice."

Goosebumps bigger than peas covered my body and I tingled all over as Glen hit the low notes as mellow as a lark. Not another sound could be heard throughout the gymnasium as all ears and eyes were glued to Glen, Esther, and Roberta.

I didn't even notice the song was over until I found myself standing there, clapping until my hands began to sting. All around me others were standing, too. Mom wiped happy tears from her eyes. Grandma beamed proudly and patted her eyes with her tiny handkerchief. The handsome interlocutor walked to the center of the stage and cheers of, *"More! More!"* echoed across the gymnasium.

The interlocutor smiled proudly and motioned for the trio to continue.

Once again, an unusual hush swept over the entire audience as Glen smiled and nodded to the orchestra leader. Softly, the trio began:

"The chimes of time ring out the news,
Another day is through
Someone slipped and fell,
Was that someone you?
You may have longed for added strength
Your courage to renew.
Do not be disheartened,
For I bring hope to you.
It is no secret what God can do.
What He's done for others,
He'll do for you.
With arms wide open, He'll pardon you,
It is no secret what God can do..."

When Glen, Esther, and Roberta finished their song this time people burst out of their seats like popcorn out of a hot kettle, clapping and clapping and clapping. How proud I was of Glen! Now the tears welled up inside my eyes. Now I was allowed to cry tears of joy! My skin prickled at the back of my neck. Glen's and my long-held secret dream had finally come true!

The interlocutor stood beside Glen and clapped while Esther wheeled Glen's wheelchair to the side of the stage. "Wasn't that beautiful?" he said. Still on our feet we clapped louder and louder.

With a smile on his face, the interlocutor took his hat from his head and pointed it to Glen. The applause grew louder.

Esther rose from her chair and once again pushed Glen to the center of the stage. Roberta set her tambourine on her seat, smiled a pretty smile through her missing front teeth and rushed to meet Glen and Esther at center stage. Glen beamed proudly and nodded his head. Esther and Roberta bowed in respect.

"My! My! My!" the interlocutor said. "Wasn't that a blessing?" He bowed to Glen who now sat at the side of the stage, then to Esther and Roberta. All around me people began to finally settle into their seats.

"And now, may I introduce you to a young girl destined to become the next super star in the field of country music? A girl who needs no introduction to anyone who has lived in this part of the country in the past few years. Ladies and gentlemen—*Liz Williamson.*"

Liz sauntered to the center of the stage. Her hair hung down in pigtails, just as it did when I had first met her on the little yellow school bus that first day of school. Freckles were painted on her nose and cheeks. Her complete attire was pure country. And strapped around her shoulder, as though it were part of her body, was that same little brown guitar I remembered her pulling from under the seat of that tiny school bus.

My heart began to beat faster, thumping wildly against my chest. Once again the audience became quiet as Liz began her song:

"Down in the valley,
Valley so low
Hang your head over
Hear that train blow.
Hear that train blow, dear,
Hear that train blow,
Late in the evening,
Hear that train blow…"

Once again my skin prickled and my hair stood out on the back of my neck as Liz bowed and blew kisses to the audience.

"Doggone! She sure is good!" I heard Uncle Slim say above the clapping.

Other performers followed Liz to the center of the stage and sang or danced. One boy dressed like Shirley Temple and pantomimed her song "The Good Ship Lollipop." Since he was much older than Shirley Temple, and somewhat chubby, he was all the more funny with his wig and painted cheeks. As he pretended he was singing, Shirley Temple's voice really came out. How silly it sounded and what laughs he received as he tap-danced across the stage! Once he fell to the floor and lost his wig. Quickly, he jumped up, placed the wig backwards on his head and continued to dance with his arms waving through the air. With each step the audience groaned with laughter.

I heard more clapping and more laughter, but I was lost in my thoughts of Glen until I realized the handsome interlocutor was speaking solemnly to the audience. "Sadly, the time has come to say good-bye," he said.

Then the chorus rose from their seats and sang a song. The hillbillies bowed and shook their tambourines in unison. And the red, velvet curtains slowly closed. Grandma and Aunt Rose jumped to their feet, clapping loudly. Before I could get to my feet, everyone in the gymnasium was standing and clapping until my ears hurt.

The clapping went on and on. And one by one the performers came forward and took their final bows. Dad winked at Glen, Esther, and Roberta. Mom squeezed Aunt Rose's hand and smiled. "Thanks for everything, Rose!"

"Hogwash!" she said. "Those kids got their talent from you, not me!"

Aunt Rose knew Mom wasn't referring to Glen's, Esther's, and Roberta's talents. She knew Mom was referring to all the hard times Aunt Rose had been at her side. She knew Mom was saying, "Thanks for helping me raise the brood!"

And Mom knew Aunt Rose would not gloat on any silly praise for doing what she loved best—raising the brood. Both women hugged each other and the subject was dropped.

People I didn't even know began coming down the aisles and hugging Mom and Dad. Uncle Clyde beamed proudly and pulled his pants up with his wrists.

"The finest show ever!" I heard some people say as they left the gymnasium.

"It will be very hard to repeat!" others boasted.

At the far steps to the hallway, three young men were lowering Glen's wheelchair to the gymnasium floor. I rushed to be beside Glen. I didn't say anything to Glen. I only smiled and walked proudly by his side as Esther and Roberta pushed his wheelchair through the crowd. Some people shook his hand as he went by and said kind words of praise. Others asked for his autograph.

"You were just super! Each of you!" Mom said to Glen, Esther, and Roberta as they met in front of the stage. "I'm so proud of all of you!" She hugged Esther and Roberta then bent over and lovingly caressed Glen's frail hand.

"You were terrific!" Grandma cried, hugging Ronny and Liz. "My goodness," she said to Aunt Rose and Mrs. Vincent, "it's just like old home week with so many from Anglin' Road performing tonight."

Dad smiled and rubbed Ronny's head. He winked to Liz and said, "Yes, all of our children were great, weren't they! After all, we are just one big family on Anglin' Road!"

Henry took a proud grasp to the back of Glen's wheelchair. "Come on everybody, let's go home!"

He began pushing Glen's wheelchair to the rear exit of the gymnasium. Then, as though he remembered what I had said on that first day we pulled up our driveway and stared at our old, run-down house, he winked at me and said, "Let's take our celebrity here, home t' our *mansion* on Anglin' Road!"

Mansion? Of course I remembered referring to our old house as a mansion on that very first day I set my eyes upon it. But a mansion is where rich people live!

"Yes," I whispered under my breath, as I stared at Glen with admiring eyes and followed my family to the rear of the gymnasium. *"Let's do go home! Home to our mansion on Anglin' Road!"*

In the dark parking lot, behind that little schoolhouse, I strutted proudly behind my family. For a moment, I paused and listened to their joyful laughter ring out in that cold November air. Above me, millions of tiny stars twinkled brilliantly. Suddenly, my thoughts drifted back to the day we first moved to Anglin' Road. I remembered so clearly now Esther's words in the Willys that bitter January day so long ago: "It's God's will! That's why we're moving to Hartford. Someday we'll know the reason why!"

Just like that first day we moved to Anglin' Road, I could feel goose bumps as big as knuckles rushing all over my body. I reached down, deep into my pants pocket, and clutched my lucky stone. Carefully, I pulled it from my pocket. "We did it!" I whispered.

Wrapping my fist tightly around that lucky stone, I lifted it high above my head and gazed wonderfully into that legion of stars that lit up that cold, November sky.

"Someday," I whispered to those brilliant stars, "I will write of our enchanted, old house and the sacred fields that surround its hallowed walls. I will tell of Glen and all my brothers and sisters, and of Mom and Dad. I will tell of Grandma and Uncle Slim, and Liz and Ronny, and Betty Jane and Bert Becker. And I will tell of Aunt Rose and Uncle Clyde."

Yes, someday I will tell the whole wide world! But now I must go home, home to *our mansion on Anglin' Road!*